the
KING
of
TREES

the
KING
of
TREES

森

AH CHENG

translated by
Bonnie S. McDougall

A New Directions Book

Manufactured in the United States of America
New Directions Books are printed on acid-free paper
First published as a New Directions Paperbook (NDP1177) in 2010
Published simultaneously in Canada by Penguin Books Canada Limited

Design by Eileen Baumgartner

Library of Congress Cataloging-in-Publication Data

Ah Cheng, 1949–
[Novellas. English. Selections]
The King of Trees / Ah Cheng ; translated from the Chinese by Bonnie S. McDougall.
p. cm.
ISBN 978-0-8112-1866-5 (pbk. : alk. paper)
1. Ah Cheng, 1949– —Translations into English. 2. China—Fiction. I. McDougall, Bonnie S., 1941– II. Ah Cheng, 1949– Qi wang. English III. Ah Cheng, 1949– Shu wang. English IV. Ah Cheng, 1949– Hai zi wang. English V. Title.
PL2833.A34A2 2010
895.1'352—dc22
2009050735

10 9 8 7 6 5 4 3

New Directions Books are published for James Laughlin
by New Directions Publishing Corporation
80 Eighth Avenue, New York, NY 10011

CONTENTS

the
KING
of
TREES

the
KING
of
TREES

T he tractor transporting our party of Educated Youth pulled into the valley and slowed to a stop on a patch of level ground. Already in raptures over the rugged scenery along the way, when we learned we had arrived at our destination our excitement reached its peak, and we hopped off eagerly.

To the side of the clearing were several thatched huts and in front of the huts stood a row of people: big, little, young and old, they gazed at us open-mouthed, hardly moving. Further off, children darted in and out like fish. The Party Secretary who had brought us here shouted at them impatiently, "Come on! Come and give them a big welcome!"

A short, sturdy man stepped forward and hurriedly shook hands with us, a stiff smile on his face. The girls stuck out their hands, too, but he avoided them, folding his own hands together instead and moving on to the boys. I was wondering why the boys' faces became slightly twisted as they greeted him when I was next. I said hello and put out my hand as I gazed at his squat figure. Suddenly I felt as if I had caught my hand in a doorjamb, but before I could yelp he'd already gone on to shake another hand. The boys who had finished shaking managed to keep up a brave front: we remained silent, trying to work our fingers loose.

The Party Secretary came over. "Knotty Xiao, stop shaking hands," he said. "Go help the students unload their luggage."

The man walked over to the trailer.

Li Li was the big reader among us and our luggage included a big wooden crate packed with his books. This crate needed four people to move it. Since we had all attended school, we treated the crate with respect and lifted it up very carefully, warning each other to take care as we shifted it over to the edge of the trailer. Knotty was standing by himself below the trailer, so we yelled, "We need three more fellows to help!" But before another three appeared, the wooden crate seemed to have slid of its own accord onto Knotty's shoulders. With one hand supporting the load and his upper body at a slight angle, Knotty walked away at a firm pace. We stood there dumbly, our hearts in our mouths. When he reached the huts and was about to put the crate down, we shouted again: "Careful!" He gave no sign of having heard us but lifted his other hand to support the weight and with a slight jerk of his shoulders, bent his knees, and laid it steadily on the ground with both hands.

We were left speechless, but Knotty was already back by the trailer, slapping the tailboard and looking up at us questioningly as we stood there idle. Coming to our senses, we hastily pushed the luggage into a row along the edge. Knotty grabbed one piece with each hand, squared his shoulders and moved away at a firm pace.

Loading the luggage onto the truck at the provincial capital and transferring it to the tractor-trailer at Farm Headquarters had taken ages, leaving us exhausted. Here at the team village, however, somehow the job was done in no time.

After everything was unloaded we went into one of the huts. Inside, there was a big bed about a hundred feet long made of split bamboo. At the head of the bed, there was a bamboo partition dividing off another room for the girls. This bed, which extended through the partition to both rooms, was large enough to sleep a good dozen people on either side. Marveling at the size of the bamboo stalks, we chose our places, spread out our bedding, and arranged our boxes.

Li Li asked three people to help him move his crate, then stood gazing at it blankly.

"What a man!" he said to himself. "There's muscle for you!"

The rest of us gathered around to look at the crate as if it were a monster. It was painted a dark brown with a yellow sun on top, rays fanning out, and above this in a semicircle were the words: "A vast land for mighty deeds."

"Li Li," someone asked, "What kind of treasures have you got in there?"

Li Li patted his pockets, feeling for the key.

It had grown dark outside but no one had noticed. As we were waiting for the crate to be opened, the Party Secretary came in, bringing a small oil lamp with him.

"All settled in? It's not like the city here, there's no electricity. Use this for the time being."

It was only then that we realized there were no lights. Hastily thanking him, we placed the lamp carefully on top of a pile of boxes. Li Li bent over to unlock the crate while the rest of us watched.

"Lost something?" asked the Party Secretary, moving closer.

Someone explained that Li Li's crate was full of books, all of them top quality, so the Party Secretary also bent over to look.

As the top opened, the books brimmed over the edge of the crate in the dim light. Each of us picked out one or two and held them up to the light. It turned out they were all political works. The four volumes of the Great Helmsman's works, it goes without saying; also the *Selected Works of Lenin*, six inches thick and printed in old characters, with light blue cloth covers and, inside, the lines running from top to bottom. There were also thick volumes such as *Required Reading for Cadres*, *Capital*, *Selected Works of Marx and Engels*, and a complete set of the nine pamphlets on the Soviet Union, plus *Quotations from Chairman Mao* and *Quotations from Vice-Chairman Lin Biao* in various bindings. Everyone gasped in amazement: how had he managed to acquire such a complete collection—enough, really, to open a library with?

"They belonged to my parents," Li Li said slowly. "When I came here, they gave me my mother's set and kept my father's. The older generation still needs to study. But their hopes are on us: the future depends on us having a solid foundation."

Everyone was very impressed. The Party Secretary was awestruck by the sight but didn't fully understand.

"Do you still have to study documents when you've read that many books?"

"Of course," Li Li assured him solemnly.

The Party Secretary picked up a book.

"What's this? I might take a look at this one."

Suppressing our grins, we told him that it was the *Selected Works of Mao Zedong*. He replied that he already owned two sets of Mao's works and would prefer something new, so Li Li took out another book for him.

We finished arranging our belongings, washed up, and were hanging around waiting for our meal to be served. A crowd of children had gathered around the doorway and we brought out some candy to pass around. They ran back home, squealing in delight, but were soon crowding around the door again, sucking greedily on their sweets. There was less wonder in their eyes and more happiness, and they were bold enough to come nearer and sidle up against us. The Party Secretary ushered in the team leader and a string of other cadres to be introduced. We asked about this and that, and of course more candy was passed around. The adults carefully peeled away the wrappers, not for themselves but to give to the children, who took the half-melted candy out of their mouths to compare the different colors.

The meal arrived during all this commotion and was served in the clearing in front of the huts. The moon had risen behind the mountains; half in shadow, it cast a bright light over the yard. We filled our bowls with rice in the moonlight and sat around a big basin of cooked vegetables to eat. Suddenly there were cries from those who had already started. I took some food with my chopsticks and put it into my mouth. My tongue felt as if it had been cut with a whip and immediately started to swell. I hastily spat into my bowl and held it up to the moonlight, but couldn't see anything wrong.

"Don't city folk eat spicy food?" the adults and children around us asked in great amusement.

"Will it always be this hot?" asked the girls.

The Party Secretary swore. He demanded a pair of chopsticks, picked up some food, put it into his mouth and chewed, looking up at the moon. "It's not that hot!"

"Not hot!" exclaimed the girls, close to tears.] – Nothing is true

We ate only the rice, leaving the rest of the food untouched. When we finished, someone came and carried the basin away. The children hopped up and down. "Meat tomorrow morning!" they piped.

We then realized that there must have been some meat with the vegetables in the basin.

After dinner, those of us who had watches confirmed that it wasn't eight o'clock yet. There was only a small oil lamp inside, so we thought we might as well sit out in the yard. Li Li suggested making a bonfire. The Party Secretary said that there was plenty of wood and called out for Knotty.

Knotty came over, heard what was needed, and went off to fetch a huge log, which he started to split with an ax. Li Li took the ax from him, saying he would do it himself. His first blow was off-center, chipping off only a piece of bark that flew away into the distance. He spat on his palms and gripped the handle more firmly with both hands, then with a loud yell brought the ax down. It landed right in the fork of a branch and wouldn't come out. Everyone rushed over, eager to show off their strength. The ax, however, seemed to have taken root, and no matter how violently the log was shaken, it still wouldn't come out. As we were struggling with it, Knotty came over, planted one foot on the log and one hand on the ax handle, and the axhead slipped out nice and easy. He lifted the ax, not swinging it particularly high as if he were about to slice bean curd, and in no time the log was divided into several lengths. We could then see that the grain was twisted. Someone brought up the old story of the master cook who cut up thousands of oxen without damaging his knife—an adept of the Way which goes beyond mere skill; someone else commented that a cook would have to be pretty strong to dissect a wooden ox. Knotty split the wood into kindling with his hands, the sound ringing through the valley like firecrackers exploding. The pieces he couldn't split with his hands he broke on the ground, holding one end fast. The nine-foot twisted log was soon reduced to a heap of firewood.

Li Li went into the hut to find some paper for starting the fire, but Knotty pulled out some matches, squatted on his heels, struck a match, and held it toward the wood. The flame at first was no more than an inch high but was soon transformed into a foot-high column, as if fanned by a draft. When Li Li returned with his paper the fire was already crackling furiously. We were all delighted, and one guy even tried to make the fire bigger. As soon as he touched it, however, the wood caved in and it looked as if the flames would die out. The girls started wailing. Still without a word, Knotty poked the wood gently with a long piece of kindling and the fire flared up again.

"Mr. Xiao," I called, "Come and join us."

"You enjoy yourselves," he replied, a little abashed.

His voice was difficult to describe as he didn't say anything else but walked slowly away. I was left wondering whether he had even said this much.

The Party Secretary spoke. "Knotty, don't forget there'll be forty more people to feed tomorrow."

Still without a word, Knotty squatted down on a rise a short distance away to the side of the yard. He was beyond reach of the firelight, but his small, round figure was silhouetted in the moonlight.

The fire grew bigger and bigger. Sparks flew off in all directions, and the heat scorched our faces and distorted our features. We gazed at each other, strange figures in the darkness. Li Li stood up.

"Our life of combat is about to begin," he announced. "Let's welcome it with a song."

All of a sudden I realized that today's journey was nothing like the kind of rural labor that we had been sent out to do during school, and I had no idea what kind of a life was in store for us. The bonfire conjured up endless fantasies and mysterious possibilities. On an impulse I stood up to take a walk in the moonlight and scout out the area we would be responsible for. Everyone looked at me, assuming I was about to sing. Aware of their gaze, I thought hard for something to say.

"Where's the lavatory?"

Everyone burst out laughing. The Party Secretary pointed in the right direction, and I went off accordingly, passing by Knotty.

"Want to piss?" he asked, looking up at me.

I nodded and he stood up to lead the way. Looking at his small figure, I found it hard to imagine how he could chop a large heap of firewood and start an enormous bonfire. As we neared the boundary, Knotty pointed to a small thatched hut. "Over there on the left."

Who wanted to pee anyway? I stood there and gazed up at the

mountains. Our area lay at the foot of these high peaks, and from where I stood, the dense forest seemed to hover over us, looking like a goblin in the moonlight.

"Is this a primeval forest?" I asked.

Knotty gazed at me.

"You don't want to piss?"

"I just wanted to look around," I answered. "Is this forest very ancient?"

He suddenly cocked an ear and listened.

"Muntjac."

At this point I became aware of some sharp cries in the distance and felt a bit alarmed.

"Are there tigers around here?" I asked.

Knotty scratched his belly.

"Tigers? No. There's bears, leopards, wild boar, wild oxen."

"Snakes?"

He had stopped listening to the noises and squatted down.

"Snakes? Yes, lots of them. And pheasants, bamboo rats, red deer, muskrats. Lots."

"Wah ... so many different animals! Should make good hunting," I said.

He got up again, turned to look at the fire in the distant clearing, and sighed.

"Soon be none left. None." _- Everything is permitted_

"Why?" I was puzzled.

He kneaded his hands, not looking at me.

"What's that they're singing?" he asked.

I made out the sound of the girls singing part-songs by the distant fire.

"It's about us rowing a boat," I said after a few lines, "rowing a small boat in the water."

"Fishing?"

"No," I smiled, "just for fun."

Knotty suddenly fixed his eyes on me in the moonlight.

"Have you been sent here to clear trees?"

"No," I answered after thinking it over. "We're here to be re-educated by the poor and lower-middle peasants, to build up and defend our country and to eliminate poverty and ignorance."

"Then why cut down the trees?"

"We'll cut down useless trees and replace them with useful ones," I replied. (We had been given a general idea of our work when we got here.) "Is felling easy?"

He lowered his head.

"Trees can't run away."

He walked a few steps forward and pissed noisily.

"You don't need to go?" he asked.

I shook my head and followed him back.

The bonfire lasted until late into the night. We didn't go to bed until the dew was falling and the fire was reduced to glowing embers. During the night, whenever anyone rolled over, the bamboo bed undulated like a wave, waking all the others up, and it went on like that the whole night.

II

The next morning we climbed out of bed, washed our faces, brushed our teeth, and fetched our bowls for breakfast, banging them with our spoons and chopsticks. The quartermaster arrived and issued each of us a meal card, which consisted of mimeographed numbers representing our monthly rice ration. He explained that the cook would mark off how much rice we ate at each meal. Realizing how precious this slip of paper was, we put it carefully in our pockets. The quartermaster suggested that we glue it to a piece of cardboard to reduce wear and tear. So we hunted around for cardboard and glue, fixed up our meal cards, and went to the cookhouse to get our food. The main dish was just as spicy as before, so again we only ate rice. The team members happily took home the leftovers. Some sent for their children, who fished out pieces of meat with their fingers on the way back home.

After breakfast, the team leader arrived to issue hoes and machetes. These we flourished in the air, eager to get straight to work up in the mountains. The team leader smiled.

"You're not starting work today," he said. "We can climb up to look around."

We set off after him, heading toward one of the mountains.

To climb the mountain one couldn't start from just anywhere. The team leader took us along a track skirting the foot of the peak. In the distance we saw a vegetable plot, the whole area sparsely planted with cabbages whose greyish-green leaves were spread open and riddled with holes. Everyone was commenting on the wretched state of the cabbages when Knotty emerged from among them, clasping a big knife. The team leader greeted him.

"Going up the mountain?" Knotty asked.

"Showing the students around a bit," the team leader answered.

Knotty glanced at us, squatted down, and started cutting off the cabbage leaves. The outer leaves fell away with a few strokes, leaving a ball-sized knob in his hand, which looked very tender. He gathered the leaves from the ground and stuffed them into a basket.

"For pigfeed," one of us observed knowingly.

"Pigfeed? No, they're too good to waste," the team leader said. "They're good with rice, pickled."

This made us uneasy, and we pointed out how dirty they were. Knotty made no comment and went on with his work.

"Want to join us?" asked the team leader.

Knotty simply carried on with what he was doing, so the team leader gave up and took us on our way.

Climbing the mountain proved difficult. Trees, undergrowth, and creepers intertwined so that at times we had to hack through dense vegetation that hindered us as we filed through the deep grass. The girls were afraid of snakes and picked their way along with extreme caution, like thieves. The boys were keen to show off how tough they were and slashed away wildly at everything.

At first we were too excited to notice, but gradually the heat became stifling. We also had to keep brushing our faces with our hands to drive off the hordes of insects, as if we were plagued with some kind of nervous tic.

"Stop slashing at everything and there won't be so many insects," said the team leader.

We took his advice and forced our way through, panting. After more than an hour of this, the team leader came to a halt. We looked around, still panting, and found ourselves on top of the mountain. Our huts down in the valley were tiny dots, but we could make out the cookhouse from the smoke that curled upward and gradually faded away. All that remained of the distant mountains was their color, patches of blue extending in overlapping layers that grew paler as they receded ever further.

We stood there awestruck, trying to catch our breath, our mouths wide open in silence. I began to feel that these mountains were like the convolutions of the human brain—we didn't know what they were thinking. It also occurred to me that if a country were entirely mountainous, its actual geography would be much larger than if it were made up only of plains. People said that the Yelang people were conceited, but considering that they had occupied the mountains between Sichuan and Guizhou, their pride probably had some geographical justification.

"With you here we've got more hands," the team leader said. "The state farm wants to clear fifteen hundred acres of mountainside this year to plant useful trees." He pointed at the mountain opposite. At first sight it seemed to have only a thick layer of grass without any trees. On closer inspection we saw that the entire mountain was planted over with rows of tiny saplings. The only big tree in sight stood alone and solitary up on the summit.

"All these mountains," asked Li Li, with a sweep of his arm, "will they all be planted with useful trees?"

"Yes."

Li Li put his hands on his hips and drew a deep breath. "Magnificent. The rebuilding of China is a magnificent task."

We all agreed.

"We'll clear the mountain we're standing on now," said the team leader, "then burn off the remains, terrace the slope, dig holes, and plant useful trees. That's the task we've been given."

Someone pointed at the big tree on the opposite summit. "Why didn't you cut down that tree?" he asked.

The team leader looked at it for a moment. "It can't be cut down."

We clamored for an explanation.

The team leader slapped an insect on his face. "That tree's become a spirit. Anyone who fells it will be in trouble."

"What kind of trouble?" we asked.

"Death."

Everyone laughed and exclaimed that this was impossible.

"What do you mean, impossible? In all the years we've been here not even the King of Trees, let alone anyone else, has touched a tree spirit."

We roared with laughter again and asked how a tree could become a spirit? And what was all this about a King of Trees?

"It's a superstition," said Li Li. "The growth cycle of plants means that the new supersedes the old, it's a law of nature. So if something gets too big and too old, people believe it's a spirit. Hasn't anyone ever tried to cut it down, team leader?"

"I did, when we were clearing the mountain," the team leader replied. "But after hacking at it for a while I started to feel queasy. Then the King of Trees told me it couldn't be cut down and I didn't dare go on."

"Who's this King of Trees?"

The team leader became hesitant. "Ah, the King of Trees. Why, it's ... well ..." He scratched the back of his head. "Come on, time to go down. Now you know what the job is."

Not budging, we pressed him to tell us who was the King of Trees.

"That's enough, that's enough," he said, looking sorry he had ever mentioned it, and moved away.

We concluded that the King of Trees must be a counterrevolutionary. It was considered rather inadvisable to talk about such people in the cities, too.

"I bet he's involved in superstitious activities," declared Li Li. "Do state farm workers have such a low level of consciousness? They leave a tree alone simply because someone says they can't chop it down?"

The team leader didn't reply and stayed silent the whole way down.

Back at the village we couldn't help looking up at the tree and wondering about it. As we had all afternoon to clean up our living quarters, a few of us arranged to climb up after lunch and take a look.

The noon sun was fierce. The blades of grass on the mountainside drooped a little, and there seemed to be a crackle in the air. We spotted a cleared path and followed it uphill.

Blindly we plodded along, backs bent. After a long stretch we suddenly saw a small boy in front of us. He was barefoot, and his tanned back and shoulders gleamed with sweat. He was digging for something with a mattock. We came to a stop, panting.

"What are you digging for?"

The boy paused and propped himself on his mattock.

"Yams."

Li Li formed a circle with his fingers.

"Potatoes?" he asked.

The boy screwed up his eyes and grinned.

"Yams are yams."

"Are they edible?" someone else asked.

"Yeah. Powdery."

We gathered around to look. We saw a narrow furrow the boy had dug on the slope but there was nothing in it. Seeing our puzzled looks, he opened his jacket that lay folded on the ground, revealing several long flat tubers. They were yellowish with white at the broken ends.

"Try one."

We each took a nibble. The texture was very smooth but it had almost no flavor, and we commented that it wasn't all that special. The boy grinned and told us that it tasted better steamed.

Feeling rested, we asked the boy the way to the top.

"Straight ahead."

"You take us, young man," said Li Li.

"Haven't finished here," he replied. He thought it over for a moment. "It's dead easy. Come on."

He picked up his jacket with the yams wrapped inside, shouldered his mattock, and led the way.

The boy walked at such a swift pace that we struggled to keep up with him. No one showed any interest in looking at the scenery; we were too focused on not collapsing. Before long, the sweat ran into our eyes and made them sting. Our shirts stuck to our backs and our pants clung to our legs. On the point of giving up, we heard the boy ahead shouting, "Is this where you want to go?" Forcing ourselves to take a few more steps, we found that we had arrived.

Looking around us, we couldn't help feeling impressed. The solitary tree we had seen in the distance this morning turned out to be a colossus several stories tall, its branches spread wide, shading a massive area of earth. Dumbstruck, we approached it slowly and touched the trunk. The bark was not in the least bit tough, and a fingernail was enough to expose the tender green inside. Under our hands the tree was warm, like a beating heart, so that we wondered if it had a pulse. Li Li walked around the tree and then shouted excitedly, "This is the King of Trees! It's not a man!"

Our jaws dropped and we lifted our faces to look at it. Its leaves were so dense and multilayered that when a breeze picked up, one side would start to rustle before the branches on the other side were slowly set in motion. The blue sky looked almost black through the chinks between the leaves, and the dots of sunlight danced like thousands of winking eyes.

I had never in my life seen such an enormous tree, and for a moment my mind went completely blank. A sense of utter inadequacy slowly surged inside me, so that my voice failed and I could neither talk nor sing—the only sound I could've made would've been like the cry of a wild beast.

There was a long pause. We exchanged odd glances and swallowed hard, then gradually began to move away.

The boy, gazing around with his mattock across his shoulder, stretched out his skinny arm and turned to look at us, his eyes flashing. Before we understood what he was doing, he slowly gripped the mattock in his hands, flexed his shoulders, and then hurled it with all his strength. It somersaulted a few times and landed in a distant patch of grass. A brown shape sprang out from the undergrowth and steadily loped away. We gave a shout—it looked like a fawn.

The fawn ran to the top of the ridge, stopped abruptly, and turned its head back, one ear quivering. It seemed imprinted there in my mind, immobile. Recovering our senses we let out another yell. As we sprang forward, the animal leveled its short tail, took a few rapid steps forward, arched its neck, and was gone in a flash, as in a dream.

With a grin, the boy fetched his mattock in the grass.

"You hit the fawn—how did you manage that?" we asked.

"It was a muntjac," he said, "not a fawn, see."

I remembered the cries I had heard the night before and realized that they must have been made by one of these animals.

"These creatures make a weird noise," I said.

The others didn't believe me and asked how I could know.

"I heard it last night," I explained. "Knotty said it was a muntjac."

"If dad said it was a muntjac," the boy said solemnly, "then it was. There's another sort of cry in the mountains which sounds like this: gu-ga. It's a kind of frog; it tastes good."

So now we knew he was Knotty's son.

"What's your name?" I blurted out.

He threw out his chest, put one hand behind his back and gave me a mischievous wink.

"Six Claws."

The others wondered what he meant, but I guessed right.

"Six fingers. Show us your hand."

He hesitated a moment, then, with an air of indifference, stretched out his hand palm down. As I had expected there was an extra finger next to his pinky. He stuck up the extra finger and made it curl around by itself. Then he clenched his fist, leaving the sixth finger free, stuck it up his nose, pulled it out again, and swiftly flicked away its catch. Someone dodged involuntarily and we all laughed.

Six Claws looked very proud.

"This finger works perfectly, it's not crippled. I'm quicker at thatching than anyone else."

We didn't understand what he meant by thatching, so he explained the process and then added, "You have to do it too when your roof needs changing."

I patted him on the head. "Your dad is very strong," I said.

He set his skinny legs apart and threw back his shoulders. "Dad used to be in the army, a scout, he's been to a foreign country. He told me that it was just like here—mountains, and trees on the mountains."

"Korea?" I guessed.

He paused, shook his head, and pointed, saying, "Over there."

We knew we weren't far from the border and gazed in that direction, but there were only mountains, nothing but mountains to be seen.

⌘

We started to hike back but turned to have one last look at the King of Trees. It stood calmly on the mountaintop, its leaves rustling as if it were murmuring to itself or teasing hundreds of children.

Li Li halted. "See how much space the tree occupies! The way it blocks off the sunlight—how can the new trees grow?"

We recognized the truth in what he was saying but weren't sure what he really meant.

"Well, it's the King of Trees," someone replied.

Li Li dropped the subject and followed us down the mountain.

III

The next day we started chopping trees on the mountain.

For hundreds and thousands of years no one touched this primeval jungle—the entire forest grew into a single, tangled whole. In its mutual concession and competition for growth, the vegetation left no space vacant on the ground. Like women paying social calls despite their advancing years, vines visited one tree to the next, on and on. The flora was very luxuriant, with each year's growth overlaying the withering top-crust so that new blades were forced to push their way through. Our feet plopped into each step, sometimes sinking in deeply.

Felling trees turned out to be no easy task. Even when we cut clean through a tree until it tilted, the tree still wouldn't fall but would be caught in a mesh of creepers, or rest against neighboring trees. More than a hundred people worked hard for a full month on one mountain without making much visible difference.

In the meantime a stream of orders issued from the state farm, all to the same effect: we were to "work harder," "work faster," "fear neither hardship nor death." The branch farms and production teams were always issuing challenges, and each day's achievements were reported and made public the following day. The heroes who emerged through this competition were greatly respected by everyone. The only one of us to make the grade was Li Li.

Although not very strong, Li Li had more drive than any of us.

In the beginning, we were rather unused to manual labor. We would take a break after an hour or so to wipe the sweat off our faces, and these pauses gradually lengthened. Our eyes would start to wander, discovering any number of things of greater interest than felling trees. For instance, if a cloud drifted past, we'd stop to watch its shadow move across the mountain; and if a pheasant darted past trailing its long tail, we'd wonder how it compared with chicken for flavor. Even better, if a snake appeared we'd crowd together and kill it. More often we'd find wild berries, which no one would eat at first, but then someone bravely assumed the role of the god of agriculture and, under our watchful gaze, calmly took a small bite, while the rest of us waited tensely, swallowing our saliva. None of these things, however, distracted Li Li in the slightest as he hacked away for dear life; only when the tree had fallen would he look up at the sky. Seeing how conscientious he was, the rest of us would feel embarrassed and get back to work, putting the lid on our diversions.

Eventually I learned how to cut the different kinds of plants on the mountain. I knew enough to realize that it took an ax to cut down a tree, and the long knives we were issued with seemed at first to be fairly useless. Had there been nothing but trees on the mountain, an ax naturally would have been the tool for the job. But could an ax cut grass? The knives were lighter. With trees, they worked if you put some effort into it; with creepers, one slash was enough; and with grass, a single level swipe mowed a nice patch.

Back in the city, my father, whose hobby was cooking, used to tell me that the art of cooking depended on two things: the knife and the fire. He used to sharpen the kitchen cleaver himself, then stand it on its back and move the blade slightly; it was only judged sharp enough when you couldn't see the edge. With a knife like this you could cut meat into the thinnest slices and vegetables into the finest shreds. When father's colleagues came for a meal, they'd volunteer to lend a hand in the kitchen but would often slice off

A H C H E N G

their fingernails and not even notice until the cabbage was stained red. Then they'd stop with an envious sigh. Later, the job of sharpening knives fell to me, and the art of whetting became an obsession of mine. I even read in a book how to lay a hair along the blade and blow on it until the pressure was enough to sever the hair. This also took a certain skill.

The day the team issued us with knives I spent three hours sharpening mine. Equipped with a keen weapon, man becomes very bloodthirsty. Up on the mountain I'd slash away at almost everything in sight, feeling very heroic. When I used it against a tree, however, I often put nicks in the blade.

After clearing the mountain for a month or so we got into a routine. We learned how to work more efficiently, but more importantly we learned how to rest. During our rest periods we'd often gaze into the distance but inevitably our eyes would fall on the King of Trees. We began discussing ways to topple the King once we finished reforesting the mountain. Dozens of proposals were put forward, until we saw that there'd be another big tree we'd soon have to chop.

This tree also stood on a mountaintop, like the King of Trees. Initially inconspicuous, its size became more obvious as the felling proceeded upward from the foot of the mountain to the summit. I discovered, however, that the older workers had started to shift to the other side of the mountain, leaving the summit alone. The rest of our group soon noticed, too; we discussed the matter and concluded that it had something to do with tallied man-hours. – Tao.

Before we left at the end of each day the team secretary would get out his tape and measure the area each person had cleared, and this figure was entered beside each of our names in the daily tally. Theoretically, the larger a tree was, the bigger the area it would cover. Beyond a certain size, however, the hours it took to chop down a tree would be proportionately much greater than the area it covered. Experienced hands therefore avoided the bigger trees on various pretexts, preferring trees with large crowns and slender trunks. We saw ourselves how the others moved off to clear the perimeter when it was time to fell the big tree.

We climbed up to the mountaintop again, and sat down to catch our breath.

While we were chatting, Li Li stood up, gripped his knife, and slowly approached the big tree. Everybody stopped talking and watched him circle the tree. Holding a fist up level with his mouth, he measured a place and lifted his knife. Then he raised his eyes higher, chose another spot and struck the knife into the bark. Realizing what he was up to, we sighed with relief and went over to watch.

To fell a large tree you need to cut a wedge into its trunk: the larger the tree, the larger the wedge. On the tree Li Li was cutting, the distance between the upper and the lower notches needed to be about five feet. Someone calculated that we'd have to cut out a cubic yard of wood to bring down the tree, a good four days' work. This perked up our interest—we agreed to join forces and fell it together, never mind the man-hours.

By general agreement I was given the task of sharpening the knives. I accepted, shouldering four of them, and started down the mountain.

It was almost noon by the time I had finished sharpening three knives. I was working away at the fourth when I became aware of a shadow looming over me. Looking up, I saw Knotty beside me, hugging his shoulders. Seeing that I had stopped, he bent over and picked up one of the sharpened knives. He ran his right thumb slowly across the blade, leveled it, and sighted down the blade as if it were a gun barrel. With a nod of approval he squatted down.

"You know how to sharpen knives?" he asked, glancing at the grindstone.

Naturally pleased with myself, I lifted the knife I was holding and flashed it around. "More or less."

Without a word he picked up another sharpened knife, took it

A H C H E N G

over to a nearby log, raised it slightly in both hands, and made a swift chop. Then, hunching his right shoulder, he pulled the knife out. He lifted it up, looked at the blade, and used his right hand to swing it back into the log. This done, he let go of the handle and called me over.

"Pull it out and look at the blade."

I went over, somewhat puzzled, and pulled the knife out with both hands. When I looked at the blade, I was surprised to see that the edge was chipped. Knotty spread open his palms.

"If you make a straight cut in the timber and pull the blade out straight, it won't chip. But the steel in this knife is brittle. If you don't get it straight, the blade will chip and you'll have to sharpen it again. That's the same as not knowing how to sharpen it."

I felt a bit uncomfortable.

"Knotty, when are you due for a shave?"

"It's early yet," he answered, absently stroking his chin.

"Take any one of these four knives, and you can cut off my left hand if you hurt yourself shaving. Not my right—I still need it for writing."

A smile gleamed in his eyes. He sprinkled some water on the whetstone, picked up a knife, and started to hone it. After a dozen or so strokes he wiped the water off and walked over to the log, holding up the knife.

"Chop here," he called out, pointing at a spot about a foot below the cut he had just made. I walked over, took the knife from him, and swung it down hard. The moment the blade entered, a sliver of wood about half a foot long flipped into the air and dropped glinting to the ground. This was the first time since I'd started tree felling that I'd cut such a large piece of wood with a single stroke. Overjoyed, I chopped out another large piece with two strokes. Knotty rubbed his hands.

"Take a look at the blade!"

Raising the knife up to my eyes, I could see the blade wasn't chipped, but I discovered that one side had been ground into a narrow bevel. I nodded as the reason dawned on me. He stretched out his hands again, palms together.

"A thin edge of course is sharp, that goes without saying." Keeping the bottom of his palms together, he parted the tops to form a wedge shape. "When the wedge enters the wood, it presses on both sides. The pieces fly up because they get squeezed out. Even if there's some wobble the blade won't chip. You want your head shaved? The blade's still sharp."

I laughed. "If it hurts I'll chop off your right hand."

Another smile appeared in his eyes. "Tough kid!"

"My knife's the best there is for chopping vegetables," I said, feeling very pleased.

"Vegetables? In the mountains?"

"Anyhow, I don't care what you say, but do you admit I'm not bad at sharpening knives?"

He thought for a moment. Without a word he handed me a short knife he drew from behind his back. As I took it I noticed that a leather thong was tied to the wooden handle, the other end fastened to his belt.

"What's the thong for?" I asked.

"Look at the blade first and then I'll tell you."

I held it up to look. It was a double-edged blade, one edge honed very thin, the other wedge-shaped like the blade he had just ground. The whole knife shone as if it had been electroplated, the flat of the blade so smooth that my face was reflected in the metal almost without distortion.

I knew it was beyond my ability to grind a blade this broad and even. Looking at the knife more carefully, I noticed a thin, faint line along the edge of the blade.

"Have you reinforced it with steel?" I asked.

He nodded. "With spring steel—it's very tensile."

I drew my thumb lightly across the blade and felt it grate; I knew the blade had bitten into my skin. I couldn't help release an envious sigh.

A H   C H E N G

"Sell it to me, Mr. Xiao." I looked him earnestly in the eyes.

Knotty smiled again, and suddenly I noticed something peculiar: his upper lip was very taut. Ordinarily it wasn't noticeable, but when he smiled, his upper lip didn't move while the flesh on both cheeks slowly pulled his mouth very thin.

"Mr. Xiao, have you had an operation on your mouth?" I asked.

Still smiling, he answered without moving his lips. "It got split. Then they stitched it too tight."

"How'd it get split so badly?"

He stopped smiling and his voice was much clearer. "Climbing a cliff."

I remembered he'd been in the army. "When you were a scout?"

He gazed at me. "Who told you that?"

"Six Claws."

He became flustered. "Little shit! What else did he tell you?"

"What's the matter? He just said you were a scout."

He thought for a moment, looked at his hands, and held one out to me. "Feel this. Tough. The martial arts grand finals. Tough."

I felt his hand. It was rock-hard: if you touched it in the dark you wouldn't have taken it for a hand at all. His fingers were short and stubby. He turned his hand palm down—his fingernails were very short and the flesh on the back of his hand looked like granite. Then he clenched his fist until the knuckles showed white under the skin. I tried to push his fist away. Shaken, I didn't dare utter a word.

Suddenly he came to attention, his arms pressed tightly against the side of his legs, and stood as still as a statue. His chin was pulled in to touch his neck. Then he marched two paces forward, stiff-legged, clicked his heels, stuck out his chin and bawled in a strange, abrupt voice: "Yessir! Fall OUT!"

He stared straight ahead with a fixed, unseeing gaze. Then he tucked his chin in again. I stared at him blankly. Then I saw his whole body relax—the skin on his forehead lost its glaze, his eyes stopped bulging, and he gave me an odd but very appealing grin.

"What do you think of that? Formal drill!"

"Drill for what?" I asked curiously.

He struck his right hand against his left palm. "Let's see. Overpowering an enemy, scaling a cliff, unarmed combat, armed combat with firearms, armed combat with knives."

It was hard for me to imagine him leaping as he sparred. "Are you any good at hand-to-hand combat?"

He glanced at me, then, without a word, he pressed his left palm hard against his right fist. He then quickly squatted down, raising his right fist to shoulder level. The next instant he smashed his fist into the whetstone. Not uttering a single sound, he sprang to his feet and pointed at the stone. As soon as I saw it my jaw dropped: the stone was split in two.

I grabbed his right hand and examined it carefully as it lay heavy in mine but I couldn't find a single mark. He pulled back his hand and made a gesture with his fore- and middle fingers. "We had to split twenty stones in a row."

"That's the PLA for you."

He rubbed his nose. "Come on," he suggested, "let's find you another grindstone at home."

I followed him over to his hut. It was very dark inside when we went in. Knotty kneeled down, reached under the bed, and pulled out a square stone. Then he groped under the bed again, looking around for something else.

"Six Claws!" he suddenly shouted.

There was a noise in the small shed beside the door, and when I looked around, Six Claws had darted in, barefoot.

"Whad'you want?" he asked.

"Where's that green stone?" Knotty asked, kneeling on the floor. "Find it for uncle to use as a whetstone."

Six Claws looked at me, winked, and beckoned me over. I bent down, bringing my face close to his. He cupped a hand to his mouth.

AH CHENG

"Do you have any candy?" he asked softly.

I straightened up. "No, but I can buy you some tomorrow."

"Can the stone wait until tomorrow?"

I hadn't expected him to be so crafty and nearly laughed out loud, but Knotty was on his feet.

"Little shit!" he bellowed, raising his right hand. "You want a belting!?"

Swiftly retreating to the doorway, the boy gave a sniff.

"Pick on someone your own size," he muttered. "I can get the stone right now, but how can you buy any candy tomorrow? It takes a day to get into town and another day to get back, and I bet you'd want to stay a few days and have some fun. You'll be at least four days!"

"You're asking for a box on the ears!" bawled Knotty.

Six Claws vanished.

"Don't be too rough on the boy," I said apologetically. "I'll see if one of the others has any left."

Knotty's eyes softened. With a sigh, he straightened the sheet on the bed and asked me to sit down. "It's a hard life for him, too. How can I afford to buy him candy? Anyway, he's old enough, there's plenty to eat in the mountains. He can find something for himself."

Knotty kept to himself as a rule, but the production team was small and it hadn't take us long to know each family's circumstances. There were three people in Knotty's household: as well as Six Claws, there was his wife, who earned a little over twenty yuan a month. Together with his pay, that made seventy yuan a month, barely enough for them to get by.

Sitting on the bed, I noticed that the edge of the sheet was thin and worn. On a closer look, I realized that the sides had been hemmed together to make a seam down the middle and the original midsection had become the edges, to make it last longer. The thin quilt, its upper side a faded green, was army issue. The two pillows were an odd shape, and it wasn't hard to guess that they were made of two coat sleeves. There was no table in the room; a home-made wooden chest propped up on clay bricks stood in the corner. The only other piece of furniture was the bed. Looking around, it was clear that all the family's possessions were in the chest, but as it had no lock, it was hard to believe there was very much inside.

"How long have you been here, Mr. Xiao?"

Knotty, who had been busy going in and out fetching water, handed me a mug of steaming hot tea. In response to my question he lifted his head and thought for a moment, reckoning on his stubby fingers: "Let's see ... nine years already!"

I took the mug, blew on the tea leaves floating on the surface, and took a sip. The water was scalding hot.

"There are so many trees around here. Why don't you make some furniture?"

He rubbed his hands, rolled his eyes, and drew a deep breath, but he didn't say anything, releasing his breath.

At this point Six Claws brought in the green stone. Knotty put it beside the square one and told him to fetch some water. Then he selected one of the four knives. First he gave it a dozen strokes on the square stone, looked at it, and then, energetically but without haste, honed it on the green one. After a few strokes, he tried the edge with his thumb and then laid the knife down on the ground. As he started on the second one he asked, "What are you sharpening these four knives for?"

I gave an account of what was happening on the mountain. Knotty stopped grinding. He squatted on the floor and gave a deep sigh. I thought he was tired. Putting down the mug, I squatted down and sharpened the last two.

"I'm up the mountain, then," I said when I finished.

Six Claws, who was standing by the door digging at his nostril with his extra finger, called to me softly. I knew what he wanted and patted him on the head. Delighted, he dove back into the shed beside the door.

When I reached the mountaintop, I saw from a distance that a large shallow cut had already been made in the tree.

"Here're the sharp ones!" I yelled out.

They ran over to get them and rushed back to the big tree.

"Watch me," I said, gripping one of the knives.

I started to cut one chunk high up and another below it. Doing my best to pass as an expert woodcutter, I made it look effortless. Wood chips flew up into the air, and everyone cheered. Much pleased, I paused to show them the knife, but they couldn't see anything special about it.

"Look at the blade," I said. "It's not chipped. Take a closer look. Notice the angle of the blade. The upper stroke cuts into the wood while the lower stroke goes into the cut, producing two forces; the bevel force presses the chips out of the trunk. That's science for you."

Li Li took the knife from me and examined it carefully. "Sounds reasonable. Let's have a go." He slashed away without pausing for breath, while the rest of us looked on dumbly.

With four knives between us, the work went very fast. By the afternoon, the tree had been cut halfway through.

"Let's set a record by felling it today," Li Li said cheerfully.

We were all consumed by excitement, and I was inspired to take two knives back down for re-sharpening. At the foot of the mountain I saw Knotty in the vegetable field.

"Mr. Xiao!" I shouted. "We'll have the tree down today!"

Knotty waited calmly for me to come nearer. He said nothing. As I was about to continue I sensed some reserve in his manner and toned down my enthusiasm.

"Believe it or not, it's all due to your method!"

He still made no comment but let his gaze wander, and then squatted down to tend his cabbages. I returned to the village. While I was sharpening the knives, I noticed him passing by in the distance, carrying the cabbages on a shoulder pole.

IV

As it was about time to quit for the day, the sun sank behind the distant mountains, giving the sky a soft glow. The moon rose from the other side of the earth, very large and a dusky yellow color. We started to slowly make our way down the mountain when Li Li said, "Leave if you want. I'm staying here till I've felled the tree."

We could see that the great tree was ready to fall, so we said we'd stay till it was down, too, and continued to take turns chopping. The gash in the trunk was large and deep, brighter than the sky in the dusk. I imagined it wouldn't take long to finish the job, and walked off to find a place to pee.

It had become very still on the mountain and the air had grown cooler. I walked toward the dusky yellow moon into some tall grass. Just as I was about to go I gave a start—beyond the patch of grass I could make out a short upright figure. The moonlight fell on his shoulders so that he was just a dark silhouette. I pulled myself together and walked over, asking who was there.

It was Knotty.

It occurred to me that Knotty had always been assigned to the vegetable field and was never seen up on the mountain. I couldn't help feeling somewhat disconcerted.

"It's time to stop work, Mr. Xiao," I said.

Knotty turned and looked at me quietly but said nothing. I turned my back to him and was starting to pee when I heard cheers. Realizing that the tree was about to fall, I dashed out from the grass cover and ran over.

The others had backed away. The great tree seemed to have lifted its foot but was still upright: it hadn't fallen, nor was there a sound. The sky had grown dark, and the branches and leaves formed a single black shape, blank and motionless, as if stunned. For a moment I was mystified; then I heard two snapping sounds, but when I looked, the tree was still motionless. Then came three more cracks, then a fourth, but the tree didn't tip; only the leaves trembled a little.

Li Li took a couple of steps toward the tree but halted when we cried out. Time passed and there was still no movement from the tree—the great slash seemed to stare at us in the darkness like an eye. Li Li took a step nearer. All of sudden there was a rending crack as if the mountain were coughing. The crown of the tree slowly began to move. I felt as if the sky was tilting and automatically parted my feet. As the crown moved faster and faster, leaves and twigs began to float down and the tree coughed as if gasping for breath. Then the sky became lighter.

Our hearts sank. Unexpectedly everything was silent again. The tree had obviously fallen but without making a great noise. We felt as if we were dreaming, it was so strange, and just as we were about to draw closer, we heard someone behind us yell, "Hey!"

We turned around and saw Knotty standing there quietly, unsure if it was his voice. Seeing we had frozen, Knotty strode through the undergrowth, straight up to the tree, not looking at any of us. We followed him, but he turned sharply and raised a hand. We realized it was dangerous and stopped again.

Knotty cautiously walked around the tree, not making a sound. Li Li stepped forward slowly, followed by the rest of us, our curiosity mixed with fear.

It turned out the tree was leaning at a low angle from the ground, entangled in a mass of creepers pulled tight by the surrounding trees. Binding the tree from all directions, these creepers were stretched taut as bowstrings, making a faint hum. Suddenly there was a sharp crack as a creeper snapped, whipped high into the air, and dropped. The huge tree shook as we turned and fled. We stopped some distance away. When we looked back, the tree was still again and Knotty was standing beside it alone. We dared not move closer. We were even more fearful of making a sound in case the noise disrupted the tree's balance and injured him as it fell.

Knotty stood watching. After a minute or two passed, he walked around the tree again, keeping absolutely silent. Finally he paused and slowly drew a knife from behind his back. It was the same double-bladed knife attached by the thong. He bent his right knee slightly, leaned to the right, and then abruptly straightened up. In a flash the knife shot up in the air. It seemed to hover at the top of its stroke, and before we could see what was happening, a creeper had sprung up and then drifted down further off. At the same time we heard a snap and the whole mountain seemed to quake. Hastily drawing back, we heard from a distance a series of cracks as one by one the creepers flew into the air. Finally the great tree hit the ground, sprang back up instantly, touched down again, bounced twice more, then rolled over in the dark, finally coming to a rest. The whole world turned silent.

We were stunned, unable to speak. We looked for Knotty but couldn't find him. We were starting to panic when he stood up slowly about ten feet away from where he had been standing before. We let out a yell and rushed over, but he turned around and checked us with a shout. He softly pulled the thong back, retrieving the knife from among the leaves and branches. Searching around him, he raised his hand and wherever the knife fell a branch or creeper would be severed. The tree jerked a few more times and then lay completely still.

The breeze felt chilly. As I recovered my senses I realized I was bathed in a cold sweat. I noticed that the others also looked subdued, and when they started to talk, they kept their voices low. Knotty Xiao put his knife away and looked around.

"Let's go down," he said, walking away.

Our spirits began to rise as we followed after him. We were all quite worked up, exaggerating the danger and teasing each other as we slowly made our way back. It was even darker now, and the moon was no longer yellow but shone with a bluish white light, making an otherworldly scene of the severed trees covering the mountainside.

Knotty remained silent. When we reached the foot of the mountain he still had nothing to say. As we neared the village we could see from a distance that the door to his hut was open, the light from an oil lamp framing a child in the doorway—it must have been Six Claws. Knotty walked home despondently, and the child ducked out of sight.

v

Back in our hut we changed and washed, our minds still on the great tree. Remembering the candy for Six Claws, I asked the others if they had any left. Everyone said no and laughed at me for being so greedy. Ignoring them, I asked the girls on the other side of the bamboo partition but heard only the splash of water—no one answered. The boys laughed at me again.

"Knotty's son Six Claws wanted some candy and I promised to bring him some," I said. "If anyone has a piece, just hand it over, or else shut the fuck up."

They fell silent, then one by one said that they really didn't have any left.

I was sorry I had asked in front of everyone. Over the past month we had gotten used to roughing it. We learned to eat the extra-hot food, now even complained that there wasn't enough of it; there was very little cooking oil available and the only snacks were pickles the girls stored away. The goodies we brought from the city were so precious that their owners hid them. Often someone would secretly stuff a sweet under his tongue during the night, and five minutes later, cover his head to swallow the saliva. Rats, who are very intelligent creatures, would naturally come and lick his lips. If anyone screamed in the night and swore at a rat, the rest of us would crack up and suggest with great concern that he put a hot pepper in his mouth to keep the rats away.

I wasn't able to bring any special food with me, so I had to swallow my desires and eat ravenously in our mess hall. This way I actually felt less of a burden. Now I was irritated when the others laughed at me for being greedy. I secretly made up my mind to ask for leave to go into town and buy some candy for Six Claws.

After we finished dinner we sat under the oil lamp in the hut, chatting. A few girls joined us. Someone brought up the movies we used to see, rambling on about the idealistic love stories that were portrayed. More girls came over to sit and listen.

I was trying to figure out the best way to ask for leave when I felt someone tugging at my sleeve. I looked over at Li Li, who nodded his head at me and left. I got to my feet and followed him. In the moonlight he walked some distance away from the hut and stood waiting for me, watching the moon. When I joined him he asked without looking at me, "You really wanted that candy for Six Claws?"

Feeling my throat thicken, I released a long sigh of exasperation. I turned and walked away with an expression of contempt on my face, not saying a word.

"Come back!" he called after me.

"What's the point of staying outside?" I asked.

He walked over, took my hand, and pressed two hard lumps into my palm.

I looked at Li Li.

"They're not mine, you know," he said uneasily.

Li Li was, as a rule, very strict with himself. We would often find him lost in thought, watch him heave a worried sigh, swallow hard, focus his gaze into the distance, and vent his thoughts. For instance, "Greatness is fortitude," he would remark, or "Fortitude is integrity," or "A great cause fosters great men." At such moments we'd look at him in embarrassment, but since we felt obliged to be serious, we'd remain silent.

The girls in particular admired Li Li but none of them knew how to draw his attention. A few tried to substitute innocence for gravity, as if regressing into childhood. I had reached the age where I was interested in girls and sometimes tried to please them, but they always seemed to prefer Li Li to me, which made me think that educated females weren't interested in me. This was quite disheartening. For a while I tried to look meditative, and it actually paid off, but it was too tiring for me to keep up such appearances. The candy must have been a token of affection from one of the girls, so without saying anything I turned and set out for Knotty's distant hut.

The moon cast a pale white light on the ground, illuminating everything around me, but in my haste I tripped over some stones. Finally approaching the hut, I saw a light in the shed by the door. I stood by the door and looked inside. Six Claws was bent over a small square table, reading—his head close to the oil lamp, his body casting a large shadow behind him. In the shadow sat two indistinct figures. Hearing a movement, Six Claws stared at the door and recognized me in a flash.

"Uncle!" he called out happily.

Stepping inside, I saw that one of the figures in the shadow was the team leader, the other Knotty's wife. The team leader stood up when he saw me.

"I've got to go," he said, "the rest of you stay."

"Stay a bit longer, don't be in such a hurry," Knotty's wife said in a low voice.

"I was just dropping by," I said.

Averting his eyes, the team leader mumbled something, slowly sat down again, and put his hands on his knees.

The atmosphere felt awkward, as if I had come at a bad moment. Remembering the candy in my hand, I squatted down.

"What are you reading, Six Claws?" I asked.

Six Claws rather shyly licked his lower lip with his small tongue and pushed over a book. Seeing me squat, Knotty's wife hastily passed over the stool under her own bottom, urging me to sit. I politely refused, bringing my attention back to Six Claw's book. Knotty's wife, still pressing the stool on me, ferreted about for something else to sit on. The oil lamp began to sway. When everybody was finally seated, I picked up the book Six Claws was reading and, flipping through the pages full of pictures, noticed that the first and last pages were missing.

"Read it to me," asked Six Claws.

I began to read out the captions beneath the images. After several pages I realized it was a scene from *The Water Margin* where Song Jiang kills his wife.

"What are this man and this woman doing here?" Six Claws asked anxiously, pointing at one of the pictures. "I know this man killed this woman, but what for?"

In the city these books were classed as one of the Four Olds and had disappeared without a trace. I never expected to come across a copy here in the wilds; beneath the dim lamplight, the book seemed like a remote memory. I felt the exhaustion of the past few years of revolution in contrast to this old story of murder that was like an unhurried ballad, comforting people. While I was lost in thought, Six Claws gave me a sly wink, put his small hand on the back of mine, and smiled.

"Shall I guess what's in your hand, Uncle?"

Forgetting that my hand was still closed, I smiled back at him. "You're smarter than a rat. There's no need to guess."

I turned my hand over and opened it. He hunched his shoulders and reached up to grab the candy, but then stopped, let his hands drop, grasped his ankles, and turned to look at his mother. The team leader and his mother both looked at the candy in my hand; they smiled but said nothing.

"They're for you, Six Claws," I said.

"No, keep them for yourself," Knotty's wife said hastily.

Six Claws glanced across at me then lowered his head. I slapped the candy down on the table and the lamp jumped.

"Take them, Six Claws!" I said.

He looked at his mother again.

"All right," she said quietly. "But don't gobble them all at once."

Six Claws reached for the candy. Holding them up to the lamp for inspection, he gave them a sniff. Then, keeping one clenched in his left hand, he carefully unwrapped the other. The extra finger on his right hand stuck out, quivering a little. He put the lump in his mouth, shut it tight, and stared dumbly at the lamp. The next instant he turned to face to me, his eyes sparkling.

"How many pieces did you eat the day we arrived?" I asked.

He spat out the candy onto the wrapper. "Dad won't let me ask other people for things."

"His father's as stubborn as a mule, he'll come to a sorry end," Knotty's wife said with a smile.

The team leader stared vacantly at the boy, sighed, and stood up to go. "Tell Knotty to visit me when he gets back."

"Where is he?" I asked.

"He's out hunting," Six Claws said cheerfully. "He'll get someone to take the catch to town, and we'll have money."

He carefully rewrapped the candy and held it with the other in his left hand. Knotty's wife murmured for the team leader to stay longer as she saw him out.

The team leader paused at the door. "Has Knotty said anything to any of you?" he asked suddenly.

I saw he was looking at me but didn't understand what he was getting at. Instinctively I shook my head and he left.

Six Claws chattered happily to me but I was wondering what the team leader had meant and didn't feel like talking any more. I said goodnight to Six Claws and his mother and started back for the hut.

The moonlight was still very bright. I paused in the yard and gazed around. The trees on the mountains within my range of vision had all been felled and lay about like corpses, stripped of the mystery they had evoked when I had arrived. Somewhere a muntjac uttered a few raucous cries—I wondered if Knotty was listening. With the mountain slopes in such a state of upheaval, I thought the muntjac might not be able to find his usual trails. Feeling the cold air seep through my pants, I walked back to the hut and went to bed.

VI

All the trees on the mountain were cleared at last, making the sun particularly dazzling each morning. Work eased off and I applied for leave to go into town, buy some treats, and relax. I set off before daybreak and walked three miles along a mountain path to hitch a ride at the branch farm. I ended up squeezing onto a tractor, which took a good five hours to reach our destination.

Everywhere along the road you could see mountains stripped by felling, like badly shaven heads, totally unlike the scenery at the time of our arrival. The people on the tractor talked about burning the slopes off in a couple of weeks. Burning off in previous years had been small-scale stuff, but this year it'd be spectacular.

The first thing to do in town, naturally, was to buy candy. I couldn't help eating a few pieces right away, which made me as thirsty as if I had been eating salt. I roamed up and down the streets looking for water. Later I carefully sampled the various restaurants in town, and bought a ticket for a film, one of the model Beijing operas adapted for the screen. The tunes were so familiar that the audience would join in at the well-known arias. I couldn't resist popping a few more candies in the darkness. Eventually I felt this was a ridiculous waste, and saved the rest. I spent two days idling in this way before taking the tractor back to the mountains again.

As I approached the team along the mountain path, I could see people digging with their mattocks in the distance. It turned out to be some Educated Youth making a firebreak.

"What kind of treats did you buy?" they asked as soon as they noticed me.

"Candy," I answered in high spirits.

Everyone stretched out their hands for one.

"I bought them for Six Claws."

"Knotty's in trouble," someone then said.

"Why? What happened?" I asked in alarm.

They put down their mattocks and spoke in a state of great excitement.

Knotty was originally from the mountains of Guizhou and had joined the army as a young man straight from home. The army saw he was brave, tough, and a good climber, so he was made a scout. He did very well at the army's martial arts grand finals in '62 and was promoted to squad leader. At the time, a neighboring nation, unable to handle the depredations of a gang of antigovernment rebels, asked our side for assistance in wiping them out. These rebels had backing and were well equipped, and it took several hard-fought battles to suppress them.

The squad led by Knotty was appointed the spearhead of penetrating the rebels' base. Knotty forced his seven or eight men on a round-the-clock march. Circling and weaving, they made their way to the rebels' headquarters, situated on top of a sheer cliff and of course heavily defended. But scaling cliffs was Knotty's specialty. He and his men climbed up the hundred and fifty foot high cliff, hanging on only by their fingertips. The rebels were taken by surprise and were killed without a single shot being fired.

Knotty ordered his men to contact their own side with the rebels' radio. The command post then ordered him to return and bring the radio back. Knotty and a young soldier from Sichuan carried the radio on their shoulders. The radio wasn't light; along the way they became exhausted and dehydrated. As it happened the road crossed high over the mountains where there was no water, and they were afraid to delay their mission by looking for a spring.

After a while they chanced upon an orange grove. The Sichuan soldier asked permission to eat a couple. At first Knotty refused, saying it was a breach of army discipline. Then, not wanting to be too hard on his subordinate, he said, "Take one, and leave some money under the tree." It wasn't until the orange was eaten that he remembered their money was useless in this country, though there was nothing else they could leave as payment. Finally he figured it was only one orange so they could leave it at that and proceed on their way.

A great victory had been won, and the troops paraded back for review. Knotty's squad had obviously played an important role and was awarded a Collective Merit Citation First Class. With the dust of the march still on them, they stood dirty and disheveled in the front rank for inspection by the commanding officer, who sped over in a jeep and hastened forward to greet the cheering soldiers.

The commanding officer loved his soldiers like his own sons and impulsively shook their hands, patted them on the shoulder, and straightened the clothes of Knotty's men. When he did this with the Sichuan soldier, he felt a round bulge in the soldier's pocket and asked him what it was. The Sichuan soldier immediately went pale as Knotty ordered him to answer the commanding officer's enquiry. Slowly he drew out the object. An orange! The blood ran to Knotty's head. Not allowing any explanation, he marched one step forward and kicked the soldier's shin. A scout's foot is no joke, and the soldier immediately collapsed with a broken shinbone.

The commanding officer was infuriated by Knotty's brutality and without bothering to find out what it was about, he immediately stripped Knotty of his award due to his "warlord style." After making further enquiries, he stripped the whole squad of their honorable citation to set an example to the whole army.

Knotty fumed with rage. He felt he was wronged, but did not defend himself and applied to be discharged. The army being strict about discipline did not try to keep him, while also agreeing to his request not to be sent home. Bearing his punishment, Knotty felt ashamed to face his family back in the mountain forest, so he came to the state farm and spent his days working in the mountains, where he felt at home. He couldn't understand the reason for clearing these magnificent forests—planting useful trees to replace ones no less useful. So he voiced his doubts. Knotty was then dragged out as a bad element in one of the revolutionary actions; as punishment, he was sent to grow vegetables and not allowed to interfere in the "great cause of reclamation." After we chopped the big tree, he went straight to the Party Secretary and told him that he shouldn't let the Educated Youth fell trees by themselves because of the danger involved. The Party Secretary replied that the young generals were eager to rely on their own efforts and were performing well; the higher-ups had praised them and there was no need to show concern. Remembering his responsibility to supervise Knotty's reform through labor, he filed a report citing Knotty's words as a new tendency.

I sighed. "That's definitely Knotty, accusing the Party Secretary of negligence to his face. Of course the secretary didn't want to lose face."

"Li Li's also gone crazy," someone added. "He's talking about eliminating superstition by chopping down the King of Trees."

Everyone complained about Li Li always interfering, and I didn't care for it either. While we talked, it came time to quit for the day, and we walked back to the village together. Along the way, the others asked how I had enjoyed my leave.

When we reached the village, I didn't bother to wash first and went straight to look for Six Claws, clutching the candy in my hand. One look at what I was holding and he went wild with joy; he scurried all over the place, calling to his mother to find something to put them in. At the same time, he produced two of the candy wrappers to show me. I saw that there was a hole in each one but I didn't know what it meant.

"Rats!" Six Claws said with great indignation. Cursing them, he carefully flattened the wrappers and placed them between the leaves of his book. There was gold on the paper, he explained, and they were still beautiful even if they were torn. When he grew bigger and became a farmhand and owned his own knife, he would paste the wrappers onto the handle of his knife and it'd be the best looking knife in the whole state farm. Knotty's wife fetched a bamboo container, but Six Claws thought it wouldn't work—if rats could gnaw into the wooden chest what good was bamboo? I suddenly spied an empty bottle in the room and said that rats couldn't bite through glass. A super idea, thought Six Claws, and he put the pieces one by one into the bottle.

After the bottle was filled, three remained on the table. He slowly pushed one in front of me, then very quickly replaced it with a green one, saying that he wanted the red one instead. He slowly pushed another toward his mother, saying it was for her. Knotty's wife pushed it back to him. He thought for a while and pushed it into the middle of the small table. It was for his father, he said. I also pushed mine toward the middle. Six Claws looked at it.

"Should dad have two?"

"You've got a whole bottleful!"

He paused for a moment, then pushed his own into the middle, too. I watched him carefully use his extra finger to pop the tiny fragments of candy left on the table into his mouth.

"Where's your dad?" I asked.

"In the vegetable field," he answered without stopping what he was doing.

I said goodbye to mother and son and went out. Knotty's wife kept asking how much she owed me, but I firmly refused to take any money.

"Six Claws' father will blow up when he finds out," she said anxiously. "Why don't you take some dried bamboo shoots?"

I refused these with equal firmness. She still looked worried as she watched me leave.

I got some food and went back to our hut to eat. Everyone kept asking me for news from town. After barely two months, we had become real country bumpkins and fancied that life was a glutton's paradise in the world beyond the mountains. We agreed that after the burning off we'd all go to town on a binge. Li Li didn't join in the talk. Finishing his meal before the rest of us, he washed his bowl and chopsticks and put them away. Then he sat down, resting his hands on the bed.

"Sharpen some more knives, okay?" he said, breaking into the conversation. I looked at him. He changed position, resting his elbows on his knees and looking at his hands. "I've told the Party Secretary that we'll go cut down the King of Trees this afternoon."

"Don't we still have to clear a firebreak this afternoon?" someone asked.

"I don't need that many people," Li Li said. "When the knives are ready I'm thinking of asking Knotty, he's still the best."

"I don't mind sharpening the knives," I said, chewing slowly. "But why this obsession with chopping the King of Trees?"

"Its location is not scientific."

"Scientific or not, it's a fine tree. It's a shame to cut it down."

"It's what we do every day. If it's a shame then we should stop working," someone else remarked.

I thought it over. "Maybe the people in the team don't want it cut down. If they wanted it cut down they'd have done so themselves ages ago."

Li Li didn't agree and stood up. "The point is to educate the peasants. In practical terms, old things must be destroyed. It doesn't matter, in the final analysis, whether we chop down the King of Trees or not. However, once it falls, a concept will be destroyed. The superstition itself is a secondary consideration. What is most important is that in regard to any kind of construction, people's ideology should be totally renewed and cleansed."

With that, he fell silent. The atmosphere was a little solemn, and we started talking about other things.

Naturally, as sharpening knives was my specialty, I soon had them ready. Several of us followed Li Li up the mountainside to cut down the King of Trees. I went to tell Knotty but his wife said that he had left as soon as he had put down his lunch bowl and that she didn't know where he was. Six Claws was taking a nap in bed, clasping the bottle of candy in his arms. Passing through the yard, we noticed that many of the older team members were standing in front of their huts, looking at us in silence. Li Li called on the Party Secretary, who left his knife at home, and the team leader, who didn't take his either, and we all ascended the mountain together.

VII

The sun was still baking, and hot air shimmered over the mountain. There was a half-roasted, half-raw smell to the grass. When we were halfway up, the Party Secretary stopped and shouted at the team below: "Back to work, everyone! Back to work!"

We saw they were still standing in the sunlight watching us but they began to move off when the Party Secretary yelled at them.

The King of Trees came into view. Although its leaves drooped a little in the fierce heat, they still stirred enough to set shafts of sunlight flickering between the branches. A flock of birds flew languidly toward us. When they neared the tree, they plunged like arrows into the crown and disappeared. Soon after, another flock suddenly flew out, diving and swooping around the tree, their cries dry and brief as if muffled by the sunshine. A ground breeze played in the shade of the tree, which covered about a huge arc, creating a world in which heat was banished.

The team leader began to drag his feet and the Party Secretary also became hesitant. Leaving them behind, we walked over to the giant tree. A small figure was sitting among the enormous roots. He raised his head slowly and my heart missed a beat: it was Knotty.

He didn't stand up. His elbows resting on his knees, he gazed straight at us, his face tense.

Li Li glanced at the tree and addressed him nonchalantly: "So you've come too, Mr. Xiao." He glanced at the tree again. "What do you think? Where should we start chopping?"

Knotty gazed steadily at Li Li in complete silence. His lips were closed in a tight line.

"Come on," Li Li called out to us. Stepping around Knotty, he wandered over to the other side of the tree, measured it up and down with his eyes, and raised the knife he was holding.

Knotty spoke, his voice husky and strange. "That's not where to chop, young man."

Li Li turned and looked at him. He lowered his knife. "Okay, tell me—where?" he asked with some surprise.

Knotty remained seated but raised his left hand a little and clapped his right arm. "Here."

Li Li didn't understand and craned his neck to see. Stretching out both arms, Knotty rose steadily to his feet. When he was upright, he pointed at his chest with his right hand. "Or here."

A flash of comprehension passed through us. Li Li went pale. I could feel my heart thumping. We stood there dumbfounded, feeling we might be warmer out in the sun.

Li Li opened his mouth but couldn't say a word. He stood still for a moment, then swallowed and said, "Mr. Xiao, stop kidding us."

Knotty dropped his right hand. "I wouldn't know how to."

"Then tell me where we should start."

Knotty pointed to his chest again with his right hand. "I've already told you, young man. Here."

Li Li was getting annoyed, but he thought for a moment and asked evenly: "We can't chop this tree?"

Keeping his hand on his chest, Knotty calmly replied, "You can start here."

Li Li was really annoyed now. "This tree's got to go!" he shouted. "See how much space it takes up. This whole area can be planted with useful trees!"

"Isn't this tree useful?" Knotty asked.

"Of course not!" answered Li Li. "What's it good for? Firewood? Tables and chairs? Building houses? There's hardly any economic value in it."

"I think it's useful," Knotty said. "I'm not clever with words, I can't tell you why it's useful. But it's grown this big, and that took some effort. If it was a child, those who cared for it couldn't just cut it down."

"No one planted this tree," said Li Li, shaking his head impatiently. "There are too many of these trees growing wild. If it weren't for such things we could have achieved the great cause of reclamation long ago. A blank sheet of paper, that's what you need for the most up-to-date, most glorious pictures. Trees growing wild get in the way, they need to be cut down—that's revolution, it's got nothing to do with raising children!"

Knotty lowered his eyes and a tremor passed through him. "You've got so many other trees to cut down, I'm not interfering with those."

"Then don't interfere with this one!" Li Li said.

Knotty kept his eyes lowered. "But this tree has to be spared. Even if the rest of them fall, this one will stand as witness."

"Witness to what?"

"Witness to the work of the Supreme God in Heaven!"

Li Li burst out laughing. "Man will triumph over Heaven. Did the gods bring the land under cultivation? No, man did, to feed himself. Did the gods forge iron? No, man did, to make tools and transform nature, including your Supreme God in Heaven of course."

Knotty made no reply but stood his ground among the tree roots. Smiling, Li Li beckoned us over. We hesitantly picked up our knives and walked over to the tree. Li Li raised his knife. "Mr. Xiao, help us fell the King of Trees!"

Knotty stiffened. Gazing at Li Li, he looked uncertain for a minute and then recovered his composure.

Li Li raised his knife and swung his body around. The blade rose over his shoulder and flashed coldly, but, as in a dream, it fell without a sound. We blinked and saw that Knotty had caught Li Li's knife with both hands, only inches away from the King of Trees. Li Li struggled to break free but I was quite certain the knife wouldn't budge.

"What do you think you're doing?!" Li Li yelled in a fury. He twisted his body like a corkscrew, but the knife had settled fast between Knotty Xiao's hands. Knotty compressed his lips, his face swelled and became pale and shiny, and his cheek muscles twitched. We gasped, drew back a few steps, and watched in silence.

The Party Secretary's voice broke in, "Knotty! Are you crazy?!"

We looked around. The secretary walked over but the team leader remained where he was, his mouth open and a bleak look in his eyes. As he drew near, the secretary pointed at the knife. "Let go of it!"

Li Li released the handle and took a step back. Knotty stood there, silent and still, the knife held fast in his hands.

"That's enough, Knotty!" said the Party Secretary "Do you want me to call a meeting because of you? Who d'you think you are? You're asking for trouble!" As he spoke, he held out his hand. "Give me the knife!"

Knotty didn't look at him. His face broadened and then diminished. A cold pallor appeared on his forehead and spread outward from the bridge of his nose. His eyebrows twitched, the corner of his eye trembled, and a bright drop slowly formed.

The Party Secretary moved off, then turned to look back. "You're not a fool," he said slowly. "Your thinking is all wrong, to put it bluntly, but you're under me and I'll cover up for you. Look after your vegetables, the trees aren't your business! The farm, affairs of state—is that *your* business? I'm just an official the size of an asshole, and it's not *my* business. But you're inside my asshole! What's this madness? These students, they even pull the emperor off his throne when they 'make revolution.' They say they'd leave a scar as big as a bowl if they get their heads chopped off: would you have a scar that big if you got your head cut off? Even if you did, how much would it be worth? You idiot! Listen, Knotty, when it comes to felling trees, you're the best man there is around here. I know that, otherwise why would they call you the King of Trees? I understand how hard this is on you. But I'm the Party Secretary and I have my job to do. Can't you see what a mess you've got me in? The students want revolution and communism. Are you going to stand in their way?"

Knotty's body slowly relaxed. A line of tear marks shone on his face. His Adam's apple rose and didn't drop. We stood transfixed, our eyes staring at him, not blinking. So this short, stumpy man protecting the tree roots was the King of Trees! My heart flinched as if it was being rubbed with a coarse stone, and the back of my neck stiffened.

The true King of Trees gazed ahead, not moving. Slowly his hands relaxed their grip and the knife dropped with a thud on the roots. The reverberation ran up the trunk. As it faded away, a dozen birds, with a cry that sounded like a wail, shot into the air like arrows. They flew from the great tree, glided down the slope of the mountain, and silently rose again. Beating their wings they flew into the sky, turning into black specks that grew smaller and smaller.

Li Li looked at us blankly, his spirits crushed. We also looked at each other. Without a word, the Party Secretary picked up the knife and handed it to Li Li, who stared vacantly at it.

Knotty silently shifted from the tree roots. With his arms dangling, he was suddenly standing a little ways off, none of us knowing how he had gotten there so quickly.

"You can start chopping," the Party Secretary said. "It's got to come down anyway. You students are right, without destruction there's no construction. Go ahead."

He turned and called, "Over here, team leader!"

Still standing far off, the team leader reluctantly said, "Go ahead, students, start felling." But he kept his distance.

Li Li raised his head. Not looking at anybody, he calmly lifted his knife, and started to chop.

VIII

It took four days to fell the great tree, and for four days Knotty stood watch by its side, not uttering a single word, his eyes fixed on the knives rising and falling. His wife cooked a meal and sent

Six Claws to bring it up to him. He swallowed a few mouthfuls, stopped eating, and told the boy to fetch some clothes. Six Claws, who had lost his former mischievousness, hurried back to the village. When night fell, he sat with his mother in front of the hut gazing up at the mountain. The moon was waning, and each day it rose later. The team members would often stop in their tracks, listen quietly to the faint sounds of chopping, and then slowly walk on. When people ran into each other, they would lower their eyes and go their separate ways.

I felt churned up inside. I couldn't figure out if we were right to chop down the tree or not. But I didn't go up the mountain to take part in the felling, nor did I speak to Li Li. Some of us were real activists, and each time they came down they'd talk and laugh at the top of their voices as if there was nothing wrong. Li Li would catch their eyes but no one else's, and then he'd burst out laughing for no reason. The rest of us remained silent, avoiding each other's gaze.

When work finished on the fourth day they came down and shouted from the yard: "It's down! It's down!"

I felt the tension of the past four days ease. Li Li came inside, retrieved a pen and some ink, and wrote a few words on a piece of paper, which he pasted up on his crate of books. From where I was lying on my bed I could make out three words: "We Are Hope."

When the others saw it they said nothing but carried on with whatever they were doing.

That evening I went over to Knotty's hut. He was sitting heavily on a low stool. As I walked in, he slowly looked over. His eyes were dry, lifeless, and dim. I felt a pang in my heart as I greeted him.

Over the past four days, his hair, streaked with grey, seemed to have grown much longer and stood up on end. His face was covered with wrinkles, which became denser nearer his forehead and ears; his upper lip was taut, the lower one slack; the skin on his neck hung loose. It was as if he was drained of all his strength. He lowered his eyelids, not saying a word.

I sat on the side of the bed and called his name again. Turning around I saw Six Claws and his mother standing at the door, so I beckoned the boy over. Looking at his father, Six Claws quietly walked over to me and leaned lightly against me, his eyes constantly on his father.

Knotty sat in silence. With a deliberate movement, he turned around and opened the chest, and from the jumble of things inside he took out an old exercise book which he examined intently. From where I was sitting, it looked vaguely like pages of numbers. When Six Claws' mother saw him take out the book, she lowered her head and went out to the shed. I sat there for a while, but seeing him so lifeless, eventually left.

IX

The firebreak was completed at last and the team leader announced it was time to burn off, warning us to be extremely careful not to let anything happen to our huts.

Shortly before sunset, everyone came out and stood in front of the huts. The team leader and several of the older hands lit torches and ran along the foot of the mountain, lighting fires every ten feet. Within a few minutes a line of fire formed around the foot of the mountain, hissing and crackling. The wind picked up. I turned and saw the sun had sunk behind the peaks, leaving the horizon bright. As the wind blew stronger, the fire at the foot of the mountain burned even more fiercely and raced up the slope. The bigger the fire grew below, the darker the mountaintop became. The thought of the trees, lying so quiet and still, made our hearts ache for them.

The fire continued to grow. Loud explosions broke out and the mountain began to tremble in the rising currents of hot air. Smoke rushed from the flames, then sparks escaped, reaching the sky before dispersing.

When the team leader and his men returned from their circuit of the mountain they stood panting and watched the fire.

The rumble of the fire shook the ground and rustled the thatch on our huts. Each loud bang was followed by a shrill hiss as the fire twisted into a ball and violently broke apart. A log leaped up and flew through the air, trailing a million sparks, somersaulting then falling down again, scattering countless flaming torches. The bigger logs dropped; the smaller ones continued to soar thousands of feet up, tossing and turning for ages before they drifted down. The fire by now had approached the mountaintop, illuminating an arc around the summit so that it was as bright as day.

My heart trembled and I turned to look in the direction of Knotty's hut. I saw his family squatting in their yard. I pondered for a moment, then walked toward them. The path to their hut was also as bright as day—so red I was afraid of scorching my feet. As I sidled up to them, they paid no attention to me, gazing in silence at the mountain. I paused and looked up at the sky. The heavens had turned crimson, and sparks shuttled back and forth like shooting stars.

Suddenly Six Claws cried out shrilly, "Oh, a muntjac, a muntjac!"

Hastily scanning the flames, I spotted on the brightly lit mountaintop a tiny muntjac scrambling back and forth; it leaped up in the air repeatedly, tracing a curve, and then as soon as it landed would twist around and dash away again. The others saw it and raised a loud cry that soared and faded in the torrid air. The fire was closing in on the summit. The muntjac finally came to a halt, kneeled down on its forelegs and dropped its head. We were holding our breath, waiting for a final glimpse of it when to our astonishment, the creature drew itself erect, lifted its head to form a straight line with its neck, and reared up on its hind legs. Before we realized what was happening, the muntjac shot like an arrow toward the fire, kicking up a string of sparks, and with a final leap, fell sideways into the flames and vanished. The next instant the fire swept over the summit. Two sheets of flame clashed, soaring so high into the sky that we had to tilt our heads far back to see. The apex of the flames licked the crimson air. I now understood that I had never really seen fire or destruction before, and knew even less of rebirth.

The whole mountain was seething. Amid the flames, thousands of trees left the earth and rose to the sky. Just when it seemed as if they would fly away, they would drift back down, collide in mid-air, break up, soar even higher, then drift down again, then soar up again, up, up, up. The hot air pressed in on all sides; my hair stood on end. I dared not touch it, fearing that it might be brittle enough to break into pieces and scatter in the air. The scalding mountain rang with otherworldly cries, a whole universe in panic.

Then within the deafening noise, I could hear someone saying, "It's cold. Oh, it's cold. Let's go back in."

Looking around, I saw three figures holding each other, walking into Knotty's hut—Six Claws' mother supporting Knotty, and Knotty's hand on Six Claws' shoulder. I hurried over to help, but when I touched Knotty, his lower ribcage was trembling violently, contracting and slackening. It was frightening: one minute he seemed to weigh a ton, the next, he felt as light as a feather.

With our help he got inside and slowly lay down on the bed. The red glare from the conflagration outside penetrated the cracks in the bamboo wall and flickered up and down his body. I placed his arms on the bed. The fingers of his hands that once smashed stone were now as lifeless as powder and as scorching as burning charcoal.

X

From that day on Knotty was sick and never got up again. I visited him daily, and each day I saw him weakening a little more. He had always been the tough, silent type; now he was still silent, but his toughness gradually diminished. I repeatedly urged him not to take the fate of a tree so much to heart—he'd nod slowly, turning eyes that had lost their focus toward the thatched roof. I couldn't tell what he was thinking.

AH CHENG

Six Claws, no longer playful, spent the days helping his mother. When he had nothing to do, he'd sit silently looking through his old dog-eared book about Song Jiang killing his wife; he would read it very earnestly over and over again. Sometimes he'd stand silently by his father, just looking at him. When his son stood before him, Knotty could manage a faint smile, but he remained speechless, lying still and quiet.

A change had come over the village. Only Li Li and his friends still talked and laughed as before, but after a while with a touch of hysteria. The team leader often went to see Knotty; he would sit with him in silence, and depart dejected. The older ones often sent their wives or children with some food, and sometimes they'd go themselves, say a few words, and depart in silence. The conflagration had burnt up everyone's spirits, and we all felt as if there needed to be some sort of a conclusion before we could rest easy.

One day a couple of weeks later I wasn't feeling well and didn't go to work. I had begun to feel cold, so I fetched a log and sat outside the hut in the sun. By ten the sun was blazing, and I felt the need to go back inside. Just as I was turning around, I heard Six Claws calling me, "Uncle, dad wants to see you."

I saw Six Claws standing in the yard, tugging at the corner of his shirt with his extra finger. I followed him home. When I went in, I was delighted to see Knotty propped up in bed.

"Ah, you're better now?" I asked.

He beckoned me to sit on the edge of the bed. I sat down and looked at him. He was a withered figure of his old self, and spoke slowly with little timbre to his voice.

"I've got a favor to ask you ... you've got to give me your word."

I nodded at once.

He paused and then went on. "There's an old army comrade of mine, he's now in Sichuan. He became disabled in the army, and he's had a hard life since he's been home. Of course, I'm to blame. I send him fifteen yuan a month, every month without fail. Now I'm finished ..."

"Don't worry, Mr. Xiao," I said hastily, catching on. "I've got some money, I can send it to him."

He lay still; it was a long time before he had the strength to go on. "I don't want you to send money. My wife and son can't read or write, and I'm finished. I want you to write him a letter, tell him that I've let him down again, and ask him to forgive me for going before him ..."

I was stunned. My heart contracted and I couldn't say a word. Knotty called Six Claws over and asked him to get an envelope from the box. It was made of brown paper with a rectangular red frame in the middle. An address in Sichuan had been filled in. I took the envelope carefully and nodded.

"Don't worry, Mr. Xiao, I won't let you down ..." But when I turned to look at him, my voice broke off.

Knotty's head had dropped to one side and hung down, quite still. His upper lip was flat, but the lower one sagged, baring a few teeth. Alarmed, I tried to prop him up, but his hands were icy cold. My first impulse was to call Six Claws' mother, but on second thought, I screened Knotty with my body and told Six Claws to go and get her.

The boy quickly returned with his mother. Knotty's wife was not particularly affected. She gave a deep sigh and helped me lay him out. Dead, Knotty seemed terribly heavy and I nearly slipped. His wife stood quietly beside the bed. Six Claws didn't cry but stood close to his mother, stroking his father's hand. At one point I wondered whether they realized that Knotty was dead. Why no grief? Why no tears?

The boy stood for a while, then jerked around and stumbled toward the shed. He picked up his book, opened it and took out the two torn candy wrappers. Gently he placed a wrapper in each of his father's hands. Sunlight pouring through minute cracks in the thatched roof fell in round flecks on the bed. One of the flecks, brighter than the rest, moved steadily across the room as if inspecting Knotty's face. Wherever it moved, the flesh seemed to come to life with a faint gleam that faded as the light continued on.

The Party Secretary arrived, stood frozen for a long time beside Knotty's body, and left looking a bit foolish. All the team members came to pay their last respects. Li Li and his friends came, too; they were not laughing now, and departed in silence. Knotty's wife told the team leader she wanted him buried, not cremated, explaining it was what he had instructed her to do.

The team leader ordered a few workers to build a coffin out of thick wooden boards. Knotty had chosen the burial site, ten feet from the giant tree. We carried the coffin up the mountain, dug a hole by the roots of the tree, and buried him there. The giant tree was still lying there uprooted, strangely unburned, the open stump heavily gashed. The leaves had withered but not fallen, and birds still came to alight on the severed trunk. Six Claws put the bottle of candy at the head of his father's grave; it was still filled halfway. The pieces looked green behind the glass.

It rained heavily that day. Toward evening, it let up for a while, then poured down in torrents again and didn't stop for a week. Large quantities of ash from the mountain flowed down in the rain and accumulated in a thick black layer. All day long an acrid smell filled the gully, our eyes watering from the fumes. After the rain stopped we went up the mountain to work again. The whole slope was bare save for a number of bigger trees that had not been completely destroyed by the fire—the black erect trunks with their charred branches looked like arrows from outer space which had plunged deep into the naked body of the mountain, leaving their black tails above ground. Horrified, we leaned on our mattocks and gazed blankly around. The week's downpour had brought out tufts of grass here and there, short blades of yellowish green.

"Look at the slope opposite!" someone yelled.

We looked in wonder. In the distance we could see that Knotty's grave had burst open: the white coffin was raised high above the grave, gleaming in the sunshine. We ran down and climbed up the mountain opposite, cautiously drawing near.

"The mountain wouldn't have him!" the team leader shouted.

Some of the bolder spirits among us went over and lifted the coffin to the ground. It turned out that a tangled mass of shoots were growing vigorously from the earth in which the coffin had been laid. We could see that the root system of the felled tree was enormously extensive, and as the tree had lost its body where it used to send its nourishment, after being drenched with rain it put forth new roots. The earth here was loose so the new roots naturally grew fast. There wasn't any candy left in the bottle, which was filled with rainwater and lumps of drowned ants.

The team leader suggested cremation to Knotty's widow, and in the end she agreed. On the summit we built a pile of kindling as high as a man, placed the coffin on top, and lit a fire underneath. The flames slowly mounted, producing dark clouds of smoke when they touched the coffin. There was no wind that day, and the smoke rose straight into the sky, formed a ball, paused, and then rose straight up again until it gradually disappeared.

Knotty's remains were buried in the original grave site. As time went by, a patch of grass with white flowers grew over it. People who understood these things told us that the plant was a kind of medicinal herb especially effective in healing wounds. As we continued our work on the mountain, we'd often stop and gaze across the landscape: we could see the huge trunk, scarred like a man who had fallen, and we could also see the patch of white flowers like bones exposed in dismembered limbs.

the
KING
of
CHESS

I t couldn't have been more chaotic at the station—thousands of people all speaking at once, and no one paying any attention to the big red slogans that were hung up for our departure. The slogans had probably been raised quite a few times already, as the paper words on the cloth banners were tattered from so much folding. The loudspeakers kept playing one Mao song after another, but these songs just made everyone even more jittery.

I had already seen off my few friends, and now that it was my turn for team transplantation, there was no one left to see me off. My parents had been blacklisted by the authorities at some point, and as soon as the Cultural Revolution started they were arrested and died shortly thereafter. Each piece of our furniture, which displayed a government-property stamped aluminum plate, was carted away—this being very right and proper, of course. Although I was an orphan, I didn't count as an only child, so I couldn't stay in the city as an urban remainder. Like a wolf in the wild I drifted around for over a year, but in the end I decided to leave anyway. The pay where we'd be going was supposed to be over twenty yuan a month, so I was looking forward to moving. And to my surprise my application was approved. The place we were leaving for bordered another country, which meant that in terms of struggle, apart from class issues, there were also international intervention issues to consider. If there was something out of line in your background, the Party might have its doubts. I don't have to say how happy I was to win this trust *and* the privileges, but what was more important was the twenty-odd yuan a month—much more than I could ever dream of spending! Still, I was a bit irritated having no one to see me off, so I squeezed my way into the car to find my seat, leaving the thousands to make their farewells on the platform.

The windows on the platform side of the car were packed with Educated Youth from different schools leaning out to crack jokes or shed tears. The windows on the other side faced south, and the winter sunlight streamed in, casting a cold glow on the rows of haunches to the north. The luggage racks on both sides were crammed full. As I walked around looking for my seat, I discovered someone sitting on his own—a thin, young student with his hands tucked into his sleeves, gazing out of the window at an empty cargo train on the south side of the station.

My seat happened to be in the same section as his, opposite him at an angle, so I sat down and tucked my hands into my sleeves, too. He transferred his gaze to me for a minute, his eyes instantly lighting up.

"Care for a game of chess?" he asked.

Startled, I hastily waved my hands. "I can't play!"

He looked at me disbelievingly. "Long thin fingers like that are made for playing. I bet you can. Let's have a game, I've got a set here." He reached up and grabbed his satchel from the window hook, then rummaged around inside.

"I only know that the horse moves up one space and diagonal, the advisor moves one space diagonal ... basic stuff," I said. "You don't have anyone seeing you off?"

He had brought out the chess set and put it on the small table. There wasn't room to lay out the plastic cloth chessboard, but after thinking for a moment he placed it sideways.

"It doesn't matter, we can still play," he said. "Come on, you go first."

I started to laugh. "You don't have anyone to see you off? What kind of a game can we play in this chaos?"

"Who the fuck do I want to see me off?" he asked, setting out the last piece. "Where we're going there's something to eat. What a fuss, all their whining and bawling! Come on, you go first."

I felt a bit strange but I picked up my cannon and moved it toward the center line. Before I could even finish my move, though, his horse banged down, faster than mine. Then I deliberately moved my cannon one point past the river.

He glanced quickly at my chin.

"You still say you can't play? Taking cannon across three and up to six for an opening gambit—I met a famous player in Zhengzhou who played this opening—came close to losing, too. But cannon across three and up to five at the center line—now that's an old move but it's got momentum, plus it's safe. Eh? Your move."

With no idea of what to do for my next move, my hand hovered over the board. Betraying no expression, he scanned the board and then tucked his hands back into his sleeves.

At this point the car erupted as a mass of people crowded inside, waving through the glass to the people outside. I stood up and looked north through the window at the platform. The people on the platform were crowding in front of the cars, everyone yelling—it was utter chaos. Then the train jerked, the crowd gasped, and the sound of weeping filled the air.

Someone shoved me in the back and I turned around. The chess player was protecting the board with one hand.

"This is no way to play," he said. "It's your move!"

I really wasn't in any mood for chess; actually, I was feeling quite low.

"Game's over," I said harshly. "This isn't the time for chess!"

He looked at me in amazement then seemed to understand. His body sagged in agreement.

After the train sped along for a while the car began to quiet down. The hot water attendant came around and everyone fished out their mugs. The boy beside me filled his and said, "Whose chess set is this? Clear it away so we can put our mugs down."

"Care for a game?" the chess player asked pathetically.

"Oh ... well, why not?" said the boy who wanted to put his mug down. "One game."

The chess player beamed and swiftly set out the pieces.

"What's the idea of placing it sideways?" his opponent said. "You can't see what you're doing."

He rubbed his hands. "It'll do. Isn't the board usually sideways when you're watching chess? You go first."

With an experienced air his opponent picked up a piece. "Cannon to center line," he muttered to himself.

The chess player again brought out his horse. His opponent immediately took his soldier, but the chess player next took his opponent's cannon with his horse. I didn't think this simple opening gambit was very interesting, and in truth I wasn't that into chess anyway, so I turned away.

At this point a schoolmate of mine appeared, looking as if he were searching for someone. As soon as he saw me he said, "Hey! We're one man short, we need you to be a fourth."

I knew they were playing cards so I shook my head. He pushed his way into our section and was about to stretch out his hand to grab me when suddenly he shouted, "Chess Fool! What are you doing here? Your sister was looking all over for you before we left. I said I hadn't seen you—damned if you weren't in here with our school, playing dumb. Look at you, at it again!"

Chess Fool went red in the face. "Always intruding into other people's business—can't I have a game without you butting in?" he said crossly. "Go away, just go away." And he urged his opponent beside me to continue.

It suddenly dawned on me whom they were referring to. "Is *he* Wang Yisheng?" I asked my schoolmate.

He stared at me. "You don't know him? Shit, where have you been all your life? Haven't you heard of the Chess Fool?"

"I knew the Chess Fool was Wang Yisheng, but I didn't know that *he* was Wang Yisheng."

I looked carefully at this thin schoolboy. Wang Yisheng forced a smile, keeping his eyes on the chessboard.

Wang Yisheng was a real celebrity. Within our school and with neighboring schools we often organized chess tournaments from which a few top players had surfaced. These top players often challenged each other, and over a period of time, the champion would almost always be Wang Yisheng. As I had little interest in chess I never paid much attention to these chess champions, but Wang Yisheng's fame was always on the lips of the chess fans at school, and I couldn't help but hear something of his successes—I knew that everyone called him Chess Fool. It was said that he played like a demon and that his marks in math were always among the top of his class. I thought that to play chess well and to excel in math made sense, though I didn't believe what people said about Wang Yisheng's weird behavior. I felt it was just the usual case of people making up stories for the sake of gossip without bothering too much about the facts.

Not long after the Cultural Revolution started, a story began to spread about Wang Yisheng committing a crime while on an expedition for exchanging revolutionary experiences with Red Guards, and him having to be sent back to school under escort. I expressed some doubt that he was capable of joining such an

The King of Chess   63

expedition—it was clear from what people said that he could barely take care of himself. But everyone insisted that he really had joined, and because he was always playing chess, someone had actually latched onto him, traveling around with him, even spotting him money, which Wang Yisheng would just accept without asking any questions.

Later people discovered that whenever he watched a chess match, the Fool would squeeze through to the front, and after one game, push aside the loser and challenge the winner. As he didn't look very impressive, at first players wouldn't give him a game. But he'd keep insisting on a battle and they'd finally relent. Several moves later, his opponent would be in a light sweat though would continue to boast. The Fool, not saying a word, would make his moves at top speed, as if he didn't even have to stop and think. Eventually his opponent would shut up, the circle of onlookers would stop offering advice, and then, precisely at this point of the game, his companion would begin to pick pockets. With everyone completely absorbed in the battle, who would expect their money to be lifted? After the third game the whole audience would be scratching their heads. The Fool, now the Champ, would call for a challenger, any challenger. Anyone who wanted to question his supremacy had to sit down and fight it out, but no opponent would win a single game. Eventually the crowd formed one team, a kind of hydra-headed opponent. He wouldn't be rattled in the least—on the contrary, he'd urge his opponents to speed up their play, because with so many experts involved they'd always start quarrelling among themselves about the next move.

Like this, Wang Yisheng could keep playing a whole day in one place; but later the onlookers would find their money missing and begin to make trouble. Then one day a few quick-witted people formed a discreet watch. They said nothing when they saw the pickpocket at work, waiting until the evening when the pickpocket met up with the Fool. Both the pickpocket and Wang Yisheng were tied up and interrogated by the local militia. The Fool was totally confused. He said that the man was a stranger who often gave him money, most likely out of pity, and that he had no idea where the money came from, he just liked playing chess. When the interrogators saw how foolish he looked, they sent him back under escort, and the story soon spread around the school.

Gradually, Wang Yisheng felt that there weren't many chess masters in the countryside and he wasn't making much progress. So he asked people to find some masters in town for him to challenge. One of his schoolmates took him to meet his own father, who was supposed to be one of the best chess players in the country. When this master met the Fool, he didn't say anything; he simply set out a board with a chess problem that apparently dated from the Song dynasty and asked him to make the first move. Wang Yisheng looked at it for a long time, then explained step by step how to win the game for the long-dead master. The boy's father was shocked and wanted to keep him on as his disciple, but he hardly expected Wang Yisheng's next question.

"Did you work out the problem?"

This stumped the master, who replied, "No, not yet."

"Then why should I be your student?"

The master then showed him the door.

"This schoolmate of yours is arrogant and conceited," he said to his son. "Skill at chess is related to moral character, and if he goes on like this his skill is bound to suffer." Then he spouted a few of the most recent political directives and said that if he studied hard his game would certainly be strengthened.

Sometime later Wang Yisheng met an old man who collected scrap paper for a living. The Fool battled him for three days in a row but won only one game. This inspired him to wander around town tearing down big character posters so the old man wouldn't have to work so hard. Unfortunately, one day he happened to tear down a "declaration of war" which a certain revolutionary group had just pasted up. He was caught and accused of belonging to an opposing faction. They claimed that their opponents were scheming and plotting against them and had to be punished—they needed to make an example of him. The opposing faction decided to secretly send someone to kidnap the Fool, and then launched a counterattack in his name.

For a while Wang Yisheng's fame was posted up and down every street. When revolutionaries from the countryside who had traveled to the city for political enlightenment realized that Wang Yisheng was a true Chess Fool, he was invited to meet some of the famous itinerant masters in the provinces. He won a few games and lost a few, though the more he played the more he sharpened his skills. The only shame was that the whole country was busy with Revolution—otherwise who knows to what heights he might have risen.

Once the boy beside me on the train learned that his opponent was Wang Yisheng, he quit. Wang became dejected.

"When your sister came to see you off," I said, "you didn't even know how to talk to your own family. Instead you grabbed me and made me play chess!"

"How do you know what it's like for people like us?" Wang Yisheng said, looking at me. "People like you are used to an easy life. There's a lot you don't understand! I suppose your parents made a big scene when you left?"

I flinched, looking at my hands. "How could they ... they're both gone."

My schoolmate told my story, dressing it up as he went along. This irritated me. "My parents die and you make a story out of it."

Wang Yisheng thought for a while. "Then how have you been living the last couple of years?"

"Getting by, one day at a time."

"Getting by how?" he asked, looking at me hard.

I didn't answer.

Wang Yisheng was silent for a moment. "It's not easy getting by," he sighed. "If I go a day without eating my game suffers. Say what you like, you had an easy time at home when your parents were still alive."

"Your parents are still alive," I said, unwilling to give way.

"You can afford to be sarcastic."

Seeing that things were getting heated, my schoolmate changed the subject. "There's no one here to give you a match, Fool, come and play cards with us."

Wang Yisheng smiled. "Cards mean nothing, I can beat the lot of you with my eyes closed."

"They say that when you're playing chess you can go without eating," said the boy beside me.

"When people are obsessed, eating isn't that important," I said. "I suppose people who get to the top can't avoid this kind of idiocy."

Wang Yisheng thought for a while then shook his head. "I'm not like that," he remarked, and turned away to look out the window.

As our journey continued, I sensed a mutual trust growing between Wang Yisheng and me, thanks to our common experiences, though we still had doubts about each other. He was always asking me how I lived before we met, especially how I got by during the two years after my parents died. I gave him a rough idea, but he kept asking for more details, especially about eating.

For example, when I told him that once I had nothing to eat for a whole day, he asked, "You ate absolutely nothing at all?"

"Nothing at all."

"Then when was the next time you ate?"

"When I bumped into a schoolmate. He was trying to pack a lot of things into his bag, so he turned it inside out to empty it. There was a stale steamed bun inside which fell on the table and broke open, and I ate the bits while we talked. Honestly, though, stale fried buns are more filling than steamed ones, and they last longer, too."

He agreed with me, but then immediately asked, "I mean, when was it that you ate this stale bun? Was it after midnight that night?"

"Um, no, it was ten at night."

"Then what did you eat the next day?"

To tell the truth, I wasn't too keen on retelling these things, especially the details.

"That night I slept at my friend's house. The next morning he bought two fried doughsticks and I had one of them. I went on a few errands with him, and he treated me to lunch in town. I felt awkward about eating at his home again that evening, but then another friend from school came along, and he insisted on dragging me over to his place when he found out I had nowhere to stay. Of course I had a decent meal there. How's that? Anything else you want cleared up?"

He smiled. "Well, it's not what you just said: 'I had nothing to eat for a whole day.' You had a bun before midnight, so it was less than twenty-four hours. Besides, your food consumption was above standard the following day. Averaging it out, your calorific intake over two days wasn't bad."

"You really are a bit of a fool, I'm afraid! You should know that there's more to eating than what your belly needs, there's also your mental needs. You get hungrier when you don't know where your next meal is coming from, and you get hungry quicker, too."

"Did you feel this mental pressure when your family was still well off? If you did, it was only because you wanted something good to be even better. That's greed. Greed is typical among your kind."

I admitted that there was some truth in what he said, but I couldn't help asking, "You keep saying *your* kind, *your* kind, but what kind of person are you?"

Looking anywhere but at me, he said, "Of course I'm not the same. Mainly it's just that my needs are relatively practical when it comes to food. Anyway, let's change the subject. You really don't like chess? 'How may one abolish care? Only with the art of chess.'"

I looked at him. "What cares do you have?"

Still averting his eyes, he said, "I don't have any cares—none at all. 'Cares'—that's just a trick fucking literary types make up to put a bit of spice in their lives. People like me don't have any 'cares'; at most we simply become gloomy. How may one abolish gloom? Only with the art of chess."

As he took such an interest in food I decided to observe Wang eat. Whenever meals were served in the Educated Youth cars, it seemed to take his mind away from the game and he became a bit restless. Hearing the rattle of aluminum lunchboxes, he closed his eyes and clamped his mouth shut as if he felt a little nauseous. When his meal was served, he dove right into the food, eating very fast, his Adam's apple bobbing up and down at each mouthful, the muscles on his face tensed up. Sometimes he stopped and very carefully, using the full length of his forefinger, pushed a few grains of rice and oily globs of soup that were stuck on his face into his mouth. If a grain of rice fell onto his clothes, he instantly pressed it with his fingertip and popped it into his mouth. If it fell from his fingertip to the floor, he bent down to retrieve it, careful not to move his feet. If he happened to notice my gaze, he slowed down. When he finished eating, after licking his chopsticks clean, he filled up the lunchbox with hot water, sucked up the oily layer on top, and swallowed the rest in small sips with an air of having safely reached shore.

Once, while playing chess, Wang was lightly tapping the table with his left hand and a grain of dry, shriveled rice hopped up and down the table in unison. He spotted it at once and swiftly shoved the dry grain into his mouth. His jaw muscles immediately started to work. I knew, though, that these dry grains of rice easily wedge themselves into your molars, getting trapped in places where your tongue can't dislodge them. Sure enough, after sitting there foolishly for a while, he whipped his hand into his mouth to dig it out, proceeded to chew it methodically, mixing it with a lot of saliva, and finally swallowed the meal with a gulp. His Adam's apple slowly shifted down, and a trace of a tear appeared in his eyes.

Wang was so devout and meticulous about eating, I felt a bit sorry for the rice, which he gobbled down to the very last scrap— it was really a bit inhuman. On the train as I continued to watch him play chess, I discovered that he was just as meticulous about the game but much more generous. Before an opponent realized the situation was totally hopeless he'd frequently set out the pieces again, saying, "Let's have another game." Some wouldn't admit defeat and insisted on playing to the end, believing in spite of everything they might, by chance, escape the death sentence that hung in the air. He'd agree to play on and would then demolish his opponent in another four or five moves. "What's the matter? Hooked on the word 'checkmate'?" he'd ask.

Watching him eat reminded me of Jack London's story "Love of Life." While he sipped his oily water after one meal, I told it to him. Because I've known hunger myself, I especially played up this sensation in my telling. He stopped drinking, leaving the lunchbox level with his mouth, and listened to me without moving a muscle. When I finished he sat there transfixed for a long while, staring at the water in his lunchbox. Then sucked up a mouthful and looked at me solemnly.

"The man was right. Of course he had to hide his biscuits under his mattress. The way you tell it, though, he had a neurotic fear of losing his food—but is that a neurosis? No, he was right, dead right. How the fuck can someone who write books possibly understand a man like this? Jack ... Jack who? Yes, Jack London, the hypocrite. London. Fuck him ... the guy's belly was full, he can't know what hunger is to a man who's starving."

I pointed out what sort of man Jack London really was.

"Yes, but in any case, Jack London became famous afterward, according to you—he certainly had no worries about eating. It's easy for him to sit there puffing away on a cigarette while he writes stories making fun of hunger."

"Jack London doesn't in the least make fun of hunger, he's ..."

"What do you mean he doesn't make fun of hunger?" he broke in angrily. "Here's a man who's only too clear about what hunger is, and he calls him a mental case. I don't like that."

I smiled wryly and shut up—what else could I do?

But the next time no one wanted to play chess with him, he asked me, "Hey, could you tell us another story about eating? That Jack London story was great."

"It's not a story about eating at all," I said annoyed. "It's a story about life. You don't mind living up to your nickname, do you, Fool?"

Perhaps because of the expression on my face, he looked crushed. I felt a lump in my chest—after all, I was quite fond of him.

"All right then, do you know Balzac's *Cousin Pons*?"

He shook his head.

I described the old glutton at length, hardly expecting the Fool's next comment.

"This story's no good," he said as soon as I finished. "It's a story about greed, not eating. That Pons wouldn't have ended up dead if he had simply stuck to eating and hadn't been greedy. I don't like that story." But the next moment he realized what he had just said. "Oh, it's not that I don't like it," he added hastily, "it's just that foreigners are always different from us, they live on another level. Now let me tell you a story."

He had my attention at once—so even the Fool had a story to tell! He settled himself in a more comfortable position.

"Once upon a time ..." he said, smiling. "Always this fucking 'once upon a time,' but this is how it was told by an old grandmother in our courtyard. Um ... in the days of our ancestors, there was this family, they never had to worry about food or drink. There was rice by the binful, and they ate as much as they liked every meal—oh, they were really fortunate! One day the son married. His wife was really capable, she never let the rice burn, or made it too dry or too wet—it was always perfect. But this woman, before she cooked the rice each time, would grab a handful and put it aside ..."

I couldn't help butting in at this point. "That story's so old it's lost its teeth! So then there's a famine, no one has anything to eat, and the woman brings out all the rice she had put aside every day, and not only is there enough for themselves, they have extra to give to the poor?"

He sat up in surprise and looked at me. "You know this story? But they didn't give any of it away. The old woman never said they gave any away."

I laughed. "It's a story for teaching children to be frugal, and here you are, trotting it out with so much relish. You really are a fool. This isn't a story about eating."

He shook his head. "But it *is* a story about eating. You've got to have food before you can eat, and this family had bins and bins of rice. But you can't just eat and eat like there's no tomorrow— you have to remember that there might be a time when there's nothing to eat, so you have to set a little aside every time you eat. There's an old saying, 'Neither too hungry nor too well fed, you'll live a long time and die in your bed.'"

I felt like laughing but didn't. It seemed as if a few things were now clearer to me.

"Here, I'll give you a game, Fool," I said, to dispel the strange sensation I was feeling.

This made him very happy. He rubbed his hands and his face brightened. "Yes, it's better to play chess than to tell stories about eating," he said, banging down the chess pieces. "Playing chess is the best. How may one abolish gloom? Only with the art of chess. Eh?" He laughed. "You go first."

Again I moved my cannon to the center line, and he brought out his horse. I moved a piece at random, and very quickly he moved his soldier one space forward. My mind wasn't on the game—I was thinking that if he had gotten as far as secondary school he must have read a fair amount.

"Have you read Cao Cao's 'Short Song'?" I asked.

"What 'Short Song'?"

"Then how do you know the lines, 'How may one abolish care? Only with Du Kang's art'?"

That floored him. "Who's Du Kang?" he asked.

"Du Kang, the man who invented wine, his name stands for wine. It was clever of you to change Du Kang into 'chess'."

He shook his head. "Uh ... no, this was something an old man told me. He'd say it every time I played chess with him "

I remembered the old man who collected scrap paper in the stories about Wang Yisheng. "Was he the old guy who collected paper?"

He threw a glance at me. "No. That old guy was a good player, though. I learned a lot from him."

"What kind of person was he?" I asked with great interest. "Why was such a good player reduced to collecting trash?"

He chuckled softly. "Playing chess doesn't mean eating. The old guy collected scrap paper in order to eat. But I don't know what he used to do. Once, I accidentally lost some chess games that I had copied out and I couldn't find them anywhere. I thought I must have tossed them into the garbage, so I went to the dump to search. While I was looking through the heaps of trash, this old man came over pushing a cart. He pointed at me and said, 'A grown boy like you, trying to rob me of my living?'

"I said I wasn't, I was just looking for something I had lost, and when he asked me what it was I ignored him. But he kept guessing: 'Money, is it? Your bankbook? Your marriage certificate?' So I finally told him it was some chess games, and right then I found them. He asked if he might have a look. Under the street lights he read through them quickly and said, 'Worthless junk.' I told him they were from an old municipal chess tournament, but he said, 'Tournaments are a waste of time. Look at this, what sort of a play is that? Jackasses!'

"I thought I might have chanced upon some kind of chess eccentric, so I asked him what sort of moves he would have made. He went straight through each game without stopping. He obviously wasn't one of your ordinary players so I suggested that we play a game. He made me go first as the two of us played blind chess right there in the dump. I lost five games in a row. The old man was impressive: his opening gambit didn't look like much, but his overall play was very subtle and cunning. He struck like lightning, setting his traps wide open, and then shut them tight and fast.

"After that we used to play blind chess at the dump every day, and each day when I returned home I'd go through his strategy over and over again. Eventually I managed a stalemate—I even checkmated him once. In fact, in the game I won, we had only made a dozen moves altogether before he began tapping the ground with his galvanized rake—it went on for ages, and then he sighed and said, 'You win.' Feeling pretty elated, I told him that I would like to drop in on him at home. The old man gave me an irritable look. "Full of yourself!' he said, and told me to wait for him there the next evening.

"I went the next day and saw him in the distance, pushing his garbage cart. When he reached me, he took a small cloth bundle out of the cart and placed it in my hands. He said it was also chess transcriptions, and told me to take them home and see if I could understand them or not. If I got stuck, he added, I could come here to talk and perhaps he could get me unstuck again. I hurried home, opened the bundle up, but I couldn't understand a fucking word. It was a weird-looking book—I couldn't even tell what dynasty it came from. It was hand-copied with notes scribbled all over the margins and patched up at different times. The stuff written in it didn't seem to be about chess but something else altogether.

"The next day I went back to look for the old man and told him I couldn't make out a word. He laughed and said he'd explain a passage to get me started. But I was shocked when he started to speak. The transcription opened with a clear statement about male-female relations. I said that was one of the Four Olds. The old man sighed and asked, 'What's old? When I collect trash every day, I'm collecting old stuff, right? But when I take it home and sort it out, and sell it to support myself, it becomes new, doesn't it?'

"Then he said that our Daoist ancestors stressed Yin and Yang, and that the opening chapter used the male and female principles to explain the spirit of Yin and Yang. The spirit of Yin and Yang cleaves and couples. In the beginning you cannot be too bold, if you're too bold you breach—that's 'breach' meaning 'to break.' I nodded to his words.

"'Too bold you breach, too weak you leak.' The old man said that my greatest fault was that I was too bold. He also said that if my opponent was bold I should use softness to assimilate him, but while assimilating him, I should create a winning strategy at the same time. 'Softness isn't weakness—it is taking in, gathering in, holding in,' he said. 'To hold and assimilate is to bring your opponent within your strategy. This strategy is up to you to create; you must do all by doing nothing. To do nothing is the Way, and it is also the invariant principle of chess. Try to vary it and it won't be chess. This doesn't mean that you'll lose (which goes without saying), but you won't even approach the true nature of chess. And even if you do not play contrary to the true nature of chess, you must create a strategy of your own for each game. Once you understand both the nature of chess and your strategy there is nothing you can't do. The mysteries are truly mysterious but if you consider it carefully, you will find that such is the truth.'

"I said his observations were fascinating but that there were thousands of possible variations in chess, how could one be certain of winning? The old man said that this was where erudition came in—in creating a strategy. The secret in creating a strategy lies in the moment. If no one makes a move then there can be no play. But as soon as your opponent makes a move, you can draw him in, guide him into your strategy. If he's a good player it won't be easy for you to draw him in, and some loss is inevitable. He may lose a piece and you may lose a piece. First you guide him in while looking for an opening to strike. Don't let him draw you into his strategy, but always try to draw him into your own. You must take care not to sustain a fatal loss; you must adapt your tactics to circumstances. One tactic leads to another, strategies overlap, a minor strategy offers an opening, a major strategy stops and contains your opponent, the two interlock, and your opponent becomes helpless.

"The old man said I had tactics but little grasp of strategy. A tactic could be figured out a hundred moves in advance, but there was no future without a strategy. He then said that I had a good brain and that I had put a lot of effort into my game, so that in the one match he lost to me I had destroyed a major strategy of his. He added that whenever we played thereafter it would just be for fun.

"The old man told me that he was nearing the end of his days and as he didn't have any children he wanted to pass on his knowledge to me. I asked respectfully why he didn't play chess for a living since he was so good at it. The old man sighed again and said that his skills had been handed down from his ancestors, but with this precept: 'live for chess and not for a livelihood.' To live for the sake of chess is to nourish your essential being, but to live for the sake of earning a living is to damage your essential being, and therefore you must not become preoccupied with your livelihood. He said that he had never learned any skills he could use to earn a living, and thinking about it now, this precept had ruined his life."

I thought I had understood something of the chess-specific talk but now I was puzzled. "Surely there's no difference in the principles governing chess and life?"

"That's what I said, too," replied Wang Yisheng. "And then I got the devil's itch and asked him about 'the grand strategy of life.' The old man said that there are only so many pieces in chess and the chessboard is only so big, the principle is necessarily always the same, only the strategies are different. You can keep the whole board in sight in chess, but there's too much you don't know about in life. These big character posters, they paste new ones up all the time—you can see a hint of what they are saying but you can't figure out what they really mean. If they don't set out all the pieces, you can't play the game."

I asked him about the chess book.

"I used to carry it around with me every day and read it over and over again," Wang Yisheng said despondently. "Later, as you know, I was arrested for tearing down a poster, and they found the book on me. They said it was one of the Four Olds and destroyed it, right in front of my eyes. Luckily I already knew the whole book by heart, and they didn't scare me."

Wang Yisheng and I both sighed deeply.

The train finally arrived, and all the Educated Youths were taken by truck to the state farm. The people from the branch farms came to collect us at headquarters. I tracked down Wang Yisheng.

"We have to part now, Fool," I said. "Don't forget our friendship. Let's keep in touch—whether or not there's any special reason to."

"Sure thing," he replied.

II

Our state farm was in a mountain forest, and our job was to chop trees, burn off the remains, dig holes, and plant new trees. When not planting trees we planted rice. Outside communication was poor and transport inadequate, so we often couldn't buy paraffin for our lamps. At night, in front of an unlit lamp and a dead fire, we'd huddle together to complain about everything under the sun. Because they were always "cutting off capitalist tails," our life was pretty miserable. More often than not we only received half an ounce of oil a month per person, so as soon as the meal bell rang everyone would run like mad to the cookhouse. The vegetables were first boiled in big vats and the amount of oil added afterward was so small that it just formed a few, large floating blobs on the water. Latecomers were often left with only plain boiled pumpkin or eggplant. But there was no shortage of rice: the state handed out forty catties of commercial-grade rice per person per month. Without any fat in our diet (and clearing the mountainside was far from easy work), the more we ate the bigger our bellies got. It didn't really bother me, though—at least it was better than begging. We were also paid the twenty-plus yuan a month, and as I didn't have a girlfriend or anyone at home to worry about, I bought cigarettes and learned to smoke (not knowing then that the more I smoked the worse it would get).

When the pressure at work up in the mountains was at its peak, we were often half-dead with exhaustion. I wondered how the Fool was coping—a skinny fellow like him. In the evenings when we chatted about imaginary feasts, I'd wonder if he had become even more disgusting to watch eat. My father was a pretty good cook, much better than my mother, and on Sundays he often used to invite his colleagues over to sample his skills. Naturally I picked up some expertise in this art, and so I would often take the lead in our culinary conversations until I'd have everyone drooling. The others would yell and push me down to the ground, saying that people like me were bad news and they'd best carve me up and fry me.

When the wet season arrived, we hurried up the mountain to dig for bamboo shoots and scrambled down the gully to catch frogs, but we still had little oil and often ended up with bellyaches. The mountainside was burned off regularly, but when the terrified forest animals dashed out they were extremely hard to catch. Even if we did manage to snatch one, these wild animals were lean, tough, and fatless—hardly a meal. We also caught and ate foot-long rats. Because rats eat grain, people said that rat flesh was the same as human flesh and so eating one amounted to cannibalism. Again my thoughts turned to the Fool: surely he must be greedy. If wanting something good to be even better defines greed, when you actually are hungry you're even greedier. If it weren't for greed, the eating instinct would have no scope for development—there'd be nothing in which it could find satisfaction. And was he still playing chess? Our farm was over thirty miles from his, which made visiting difficult, so we never managed to meet.

Before we knew it, it was summer. One day, while we worked up on the mountain, I saw someone far off coming along the path toward us. Everyone thought it looked like a stranger and we started arguing about who it might be. Someone said it must be Mao's boyfriend. Mao was one of the girls in our team who had recently started dating a boy from another farm, but no one had met him yet. We concluded it could be him coming to see Mao and so the whole mountain started to shout her name, saying that her friend had come. Mao dropped her mattock, rushed over, tripping over her own feet, and peered down. But before she had time to take a good look, I recognized Wang Yisheng, the Chess Fool. I let out such a shout the others jumped.

"Is it you he's looking for?" they asked.

I was very pleased. There were Educated Youths from four different cities in our team, and only a few of us arrived at the same time so naturally they didn't know Wang Yisheng. As acting section leader I said to everyone, "Let's quit early today. But before you leave, see if you can find anything on the mountain for us to eat. Come down when the meal bell rings and bring everything over to my place to cook. Don't forget your rice, and we can all eat together."

The others started to hunt through the underbrush.

I ran leaping down the mountain. Wang Yisheng had come to a halt and was looking very happy.

"How did you know it was me?" he called from a distance.

"I knew it must be you, I recognized your thick skull miles away," I said when I was level with him. "Why didn't you come see me before?!"

"You never came to see me either!" he said, falling into step beside me.

I saw that the sweat from his back had soaked his shirt, his hair was sticking up in tufts, and his face was covered in dust; only his eyes and teeth were gleaming. Even his lips were caked with dirt, and so dry that the skin had cracked.

"How did you get here?" I asked, moved and curious.

"I hitched a ride part of the way and walked the rest. I set out two weeks ago."

"It's only thirty miles!" I said, shocked. "How come it took you so long?"

"I'll tell you about it when we get back."

While we talked we had reached our huts at the bottom of the ravine. A few pigs, skinnier than dogs, ran around the yard. Because everyone was still working, the place was silent and deserted except for a muffled clatter from the team cookhouse.

The door to my hut was open and we walked in. No one ever locked their doors here as no one owned any extra belongings to steal—there wasn't any need to be on your guard. I set up my washbasin and, telling Wang to wait, I picked up a bucket to fill with some hot water for him to wash. On the way I had a word with the cook. I had already used up my five ounces of issued oil for the month.

"Have you got a visitor?" the cook asked.

"Yes, exactly!" I replied.

The cook opened a locked cupboard, ladled out a teaspoon of oil into a bowl, and then gave me three long eggplants.

"You can still come and get your vegetables tomorrow," he said. "We'll start counting the day after that, which will be more convenient."

I ladled out some hot water from a vat into the bucket and carried it back to the hut.

Wang Yisheng stripped down to his underpants and washed himself, breathing heavily. When he finished, he put his dirty clothes in the water to soak, scrubbed them piece by piece, wrung them out, and then hung everything on the clothesline across the doorway.

"You're so neat and tidy," I said.

"I've been looking after myself since I was little, I'm used to it. A few pieces of clothes are no trouble."

As he spoke he sat down on the bed. He crooked his arm around to scratch his back, his ribs pressing against his skin. I took out my cigarettes and offered him one. With an air of great experience he tapped one out of the pack, licked the end, flipped it around, and put it in his mouth. I lit his, then mine. Hunching his shoulders, he took a long drag and slowly exhaled. A tremor passed through his whole body.

"Not bad at all," he smiled.

"What? You've become a smoker too? Not doing too badly, then."

He gazed at the thatched roof, looked at the pigs running back and forth by the door, lowered his head, and softly tapped his skinny legs, which were a mass of blue veins.

"Not too bad, not too bad at all," he said after a long pause. "What's there to say? Rice? Money? What else do I need? No, not bad at all. How's things with you?" he asked through a cloud of smoke.

"There's enough money, and plenty of rice—that's not bad—but there's no oil," I said with a sigh. "Mass cooking gives us a bellyache. The worse thing is that there's no fun—no books, no electricity, no movies. It's not easy to go anywhere either. We're bored to death, stuck here beyond nowhere."

He looked at me and shook his head. "You people! What can I say—all you think of is the icing on the cake. I'm more than satisfied: what else do I need? But you, you've been spoiled by books. Those two stories you told me on the train, I've gone over them in my head many times, and actually I like them a lot. You're not bad, you've read plenty of books. But in the end, where do books get you? Yes, a man struggles as hard as he can to stay alive and goes crazy, then gets better and goes on living, but how does he live after that? Or, like Pons? He had enough to eat and drink, he could easily have saved a little, but he suffered from greed. If people didn't treat him to meals he felt life was treating him badly. People should know how to be satisfied—happiness is a full belly at every meal." He fell silent, looking at his toes flexing up and down. With the heel of one foot he rubbed the top of the other, blew out a mouthful of smoke, and flicked his leg with his hand.

I very much regretted using oil to illustrate my dissatisfaction with life, not to mention things I could easily do without like books and movies, which were far above the bottom line to him— he wouldn't let such things bother him. I suddenly felt deflated, almost ready to agree with his point of view. Yes, what else did I need? Wasn't I feeling fine at the moment? I didn't have to worry about where my next meal was coming from, and it didn't matter how tattered my bed was, it was still mine—I didn't have to hunt around for a place to hole up for the night. So why was I always feeling discontent? Why did I have this urge to read anything I could lay my hands on? And films—once the lights turned on it was right back to reality again, so what good was that? Still, there was a vague longing inside me, nothing I could put into words, though I felt it had something to do with living.

"Do you still play chess?" I asked him.

"Of course," he answered as quickly as if he was positioning a soldier. "That goes without saying."

"There you are, then. If you think everything's fine, why should you still want to play chess? Isn't chess superfluous?"

He stopped his smoke ring in mid-air and rubbed his face.

"Chess is an obsession with me. Once I start playing I forget everything else. I relax when I'm lost in a game. Even if I don't have a board or pieces I can play in my head, I don't bother anybody."

"Suppose there comes a day when they don't let you play, they don't even let you think of playing, how would you feel then?"

He looked at me in amazement. "Impossible, how could they do that? I can play in my head! Can they dig into my mind? You're talking about the impossible."

I sighed. "It seems that playing chess is a good thing. With reading you can't keep turning the same book over and over in your mind, you keep wanting to read a new one. But with chess you can play around with all kinds of variations."

He smiled. "How about learning to play then? We don't have to worry about food or drink, but like you said, it's not enough, something's missing and there's not much fun in living. Where can you find books around here? Play chess then, abolish your cares."

I thought it over. "I'm not really interested in chess. But there's someone in our team who's supposed to be pretty good."

He flipped his cigarette butt out of the door and his eyes lit up.

"Really? You've got a chess player? Hey, I really came to the right place. Where is he?"

"He's still at work. What's the big rush, I thought you came to see me?"

He lay back on my quilt with his hands clasped behind his neck, looking down at his slack belly.

"I haven't been able to find a chess player for six months. As the world's full of odd characters, even here in the mountain wilderness I should be able to find a good player. I've taken some leave to go wander around and look for people to play with, and now I've found you here."

"You're not earning any pay now? What do you live on?"

"Who would have thought—my sister's been sent to a factory in town so now she's earning money and I don't have to send as much back home. I thought I'd use this opportunity to meet some chess players. How about it? Will you go find this guy for me?"

I said of course, and as my curiosity was aroused, I asked, "What's your family like back home?"

He sighed and gazed at the roof, taking a long time to answer.

"Poor. It's tough! There's only the three of us. My mother's dead, there's only my father, my sister, and me. My father doesn't earn very much—between us there's less than ten yuan a month each to live on. After my mother died my father started drinking, and it's gotten worse and worse. Whenever he has a little extra money he starts drinking and gets abusive. When the neighbors try to talk to him, he listens with tears and sniveling, making everyone very uncomfortable.

"'Can't you quit?' I asked him once. 'What good is it doing you?'"

"'You don't understand what drinking is,' he said. 'It gives us old guys a bit of a boost. It's not an easy life, what with your ma gone and the two of you still kids. I'm tired, I have no book-learning, at my age I'll never make more than what I'm earning now. When your ma died she told me that no matter what, I was to support you so you didn't start working until you finished school. You just leave me to my drinking, eh? If you've got any complaints against your aging father I'll pay for it in my next life, okay?'"

He looked at me. "I won't kid you. My mother used to work in a brothel before Liberation. Eventually, I guess, someone fell for her and she became his concubine—you could say she became respectable. Got a smoke?"

I threw him a cigarette. He lit it and blew on the end until it glowed red, staring at it fixedly.

"Later my ma ran off with someone," he went on after a pause. "They say the man who had bought her was rough on her, not just treating her like a servant but even beating her. I don't know what sort of man it was she went away with—all I know is she had me with him. This man disappeared right after Liberation. As she was carrying me, there was no way she could support herself, so she moved in with my stepfather. He used to be a manual laborer, but by the time Liberation arrived his strength was waning and he wasn't up for it any more. As he didn't have an education he couldn't earn much doing anything. He started living with my ma with the idea of them helping each other out, but when my sister was born, ma became weaker and weaker.

"I was only in primary school at the time. I was smart and the teachers liked me. But whenever the school went on a spring outing or to a movie, I didn't go—every penny we could save for the

A H   C H E N G

family counted. Ma didn't want my schooling to suffer and wore herself out looking for work. Then one day ma and I were folding sheets of paper for a printer—it was for a book on chess. When we had finished, before ma sent them back, I looked through the book, page by page. It sounds weird but I found it pretty absorbing. So the next time I was free I went into town to watch people play chess.

"After a few days of this I started getting itchy fingers. I didn't dare ask my family for money, but I made a chess set out of cardboard and brought it to school to play with. I learned how to play simply by practicing by myself. Then I went back to town to play with the others. Before, when I was only watching, I played well, but this time when I played a real game I lost. I kept playing through the evening, not even stopping to eat. Ma had to come look for me and drag me home. Shit, she was so weak it didn't hurt a bit when she hit me. When we got home, she kneeled down before me and said, 'Little ancestor, you're my only hope! If you won't study hard, I'm going to die right here.'

"It frightened me hearing her talk like this, so I blurted out, 'Ma, I've always studied hard. Please get up, I won't play chess any more.' I helped her up and made her sit on a chair. That night as I folded pages with her, my mind wandered off and I started thinking of a chess sequence. Ma sighed. 'There you go again. We can't afford the movies, and you won't go to the park either—it's just this chess. Well, go ahead then. But remember your mother's words: please don't get carried away. I won't forgive you if you fall behind in your school work. Your father and I may not be able to read, but we can talk to the teacher. If the teacher says you're not keeping up, I won't hear any excuses.' I agreed. How could I fall behind at school? Math was just playground stuff to me.

"After this, after school each day, I'd first finish my homework and then play chess. After dinner, I'd help ma with her work until bedtime. You don't use your brain folding sheets of paper, so I'd play chess in my head. Sometimes I would get carried away, suddenly bang the pages and shout out a move, making everyone jump."

"No wonder you play so well," I said. "You've had chess on the brain since you were little!"

He smiled wryly. "Yeah. The teacher suggested I join the chess club at the Children's Palace. He said that I might become a champion if I studied hard! But ma said, 'People like us don't go to chess clubs. If you want to study then learn a skill you can use. Will being a good player put rice on the table? Wouldn't it be better to use the time to learn more at school? Tell your teacher that you're not going to any chess club; if there's skills your teachers haven't taught you yet, tell them to teach you one that will be useful later. My heavens ... make chess your whole life? That's what rich people in the old days used to do! Your ma's seen this kind, they're the elite, they don't depend on chess for a living. In that place where your ma used to work, some of the girls used to play chess to charge more. But, oh! You don't know, you don't understand. It's all right to play for fun, but don't make it your life!'

"I talked to the teacher; he thought for a bit but didn't say anything. Later he bought me a chess set. When I showed it to ma, she said, 'Goodness, what a kind man! But remember: food comes first, chess second. When you're earning money and supporting the family you can play as much as you want, it's up to you.'"

I sighed deeply. "It's all right to play now. You're earning money, you can fool around with chess as much as you like and your ma doesn't have to worry."

Wang Yisheng swung his feet up on the bed and sat cross-legged, his hands gripping his wrists. Looking at the ground, he said, "My mother never saw me earn money. My family supported me up to the first year of high school, when she died. Not long before her death, she took me aside and said, 'Everyone on our street says you play chess well; I believe them, but I can't say I'm happy with the idea of you playing chess. No matter what future you have in chess, it's not going to be your rice bowl. I can't see you through high school but I said to your father, no matter how hard it gets, he has to see that you finish. Your last two years there, I looked into that. It's preparation for university. None of us needs to go to university. Father's not well, and your sister's just a baby. When you finish school you'll have to start earning money. The family will depend on you. Your ma's going now, and I've never given you anything to remember me by. Here, I collected some old toothbrushes and made them into a chess set for you.'

"Then she told me to get a small cloth bundle from under the pillow. When I opened it and looked inside, it was a set of chess pieces, a bit on the small side, but polished until they were bright and shiny, every bit as good as ivory, and without the usual characters carved on top. Ma said, 'I don't know how to write, so I was afraid I'd get the characters wrong. Take them. You can carve the writing on them yourself, and you can say that your ma's happy about your love for chess.'

"During all of our family troubles I've never cried—what's the use? But looking at this set of blank pieces, I couldn't help breaking down."

My nose prickled. I lowered my head and sighed, "Ah, mothers..."

Saying nothing more, Wang Yisheng sat there smoking.

The others returned from the mountain with two snakes. They were very polite when they saw Wang Yisheng, asking which branch farm he was from and what his cookhouse was like. He answered their questions and walked over to feel his clothes on the line, but they were still damp. I told him to borrow some of mine, but he said that eating would make him sweat so for the moment he'd stay undressed.

Seeing how informal he was, everyone relaxed. Naturally I started bragging about Wang Yisheng's chess skill to show he wasn't just an ordinary visitor. The others said we should find Tall Balls, the team's chess expert, to play Wang Yisheng. Someone ran out to call him and Tall Balls turned up a few minutes later.

Tall Balls, an Educated Youth from a big southern city, was extraordinarily tall and thin. There was an air of elegance in his movements, and he was always immaculately dressed. Along these remote mountain paths it sometimes made people suspicious to see a person that tall and wearing such neat, clean clothes. He bent over as he walked in, stretching out his hand while he was still some distance away.

Wang Yisheng was flustered for a moment but immediately recovered and stretched out his hand, though his face turned red. After shaking hands, Tall Balls clasped his together and held them loosely in front of his belly.

"I'm Ni Bin—*Ni* written with the man radical and *Bin* with the characters for civil and military. Everyone calls me Tall Balls because I've got long legs. 'Balls' is a very vulgar word—please don't take offence, the level of culture here is very low. May I ask your name?"

Wang Yisheng was a couple of heads shorter than Ni Bin and had to look up to speak.

"Wang ... Wang Yisheng."

"Wang Yisheng? Super, super—a super name. Which characters?"

Still craning his neck back, Wang Yisheng said, "*Yi* meaning one, *sheng* meaning life."

"Super," said Tall Balls, "super," and threw out a long arm waving him back. "Do sit down. I understand you're a dedicated student of chess? Super, super. Chess is part of high culture. My father plays rather well; he's quite well known, truly, many people know his name. I can only play a *little*—I'm a devoted student, but there's no one here who's any good. Please, sit down."

Wang Yisheng retreated to the bed again, smiling awkwardly and not knowing quite what to say. Ni Bin didn't sit down, but inclined the upper half of his body forward, placing one hand slightly in front of his chest.

"You *must* excuse me, I've just finished working; I haven't washed or tidied up yet. Would you mind waiting a moment and I'll be right back. Oh yes, may I ask if your father's a chess aficionado?"

Wang Yisheng quickly shook his head. He tried to speak but only managed a gasp.

"Super, super," Ni Bin said. "Well, I'll be right back."

"Tall Balls, come and have some snake after you've cleaned up," I said.

"That's not necessary, not necessary," he said, withdrawing. "All right then, all right."

Everyone burst out laughing.

"Are you coming or not?" they yelled out after him. "What's 'not necessary, all right' supposed to mean?"

"Of course I want some snake," Ni Bin said from outside the door. "I'll need to use my *brains* if we're going to play chess."

Laughing at Tall Balls, the team members shut the door, stripped off their underpants, and washed themselves from head to foot, making cracks about each other's bodies. Wang Yisheng sat on the bed thinking who knows what, keeping out of their way as they rubbed themselves dry.

"Don't mind Tall Balls," I said to Wang Yisheng, tearing off the snake heads, "he's just a smart ass."

"If your friend here really knows a thing or two," someone said to me, "we'll have a great game today. Tall Balls' father really is quite well known back home."

"Fathers are fathers, sons are sons," someone else said. "Is chess something you can inherit?"

"There are some terrific players who have inherited their skills," Wang Yisheng said. "You can't sneeze at strategies that have been in the family for generations. We'll see when we start playing." As he spoke he rubbed his hands and his face brightened.

I hung up the snakes, skinned them, and laid the flayed meat on the chopping board. Slicing the bodies open with a bamboo knife, but not cutting them into pieces, I carefully lined a big bowl with the meat, placed the bowl in a pot, and poured some water into the pot.

"Has everyone finished washing up? I'm going to open the door!"

Everyone hastily put on their underwear. I went outside and laid out three clay bricks on the ground, heaped some kindling between them, then stood the pot on the bricks, shooing the pigs away.

"Who's going to keep an eye on this? Don't let the pigs knock it over. Take it off ten minutes after it starts to boil." I went back inside to prepare the eggplant.

One of the others had cleaned out the washbasin and gone to the cookhouse where he picked up four or five catties of boiled rice and a small platter of boiled eggplant. He also brought back one spring onion, two cloves of wild garlic, and a small piece of ginger. I said that we still needed salt, so someone else ran off and fetched a piece, pounded it on a piece of paper and put it aside.

Tall Balls approached, a black wooden box clutched in his hands.

"Might you have any soy paste, Tall Balls?" I asked.

He hesitated a moment, then turned and went back.

"And bring some vinegar crystals if you've got any!" I yelled out again.

When the snake was ready, I carried the pot inside and lifted the lid off. A big cloud of steam rushed out with a savory odor, but instead of drawing back everyone waited until their vision cleared and then gasped in admiration. Two large snakes were coiled gleaming in the bowl. I quickly lifted the bowl out and blew on my fingers.

"Let your stomach juices flow!" I said.

Wang Yisheng pushed forward to look.

"How can we eat them whole?" he asked.

"Snake meat mustn't come in contact with iron," I said. "If it does it gets tainted. Instead of cutting it up you take shreds of it with your chopsticks and dip it into the seasoning." I put the chopped eggplant into the pot to steam.

Tall Balls came in, carrying a small piece of soy paste wrapped in paper and a few white crystals wrapped in another piece of paper. I asked him about the crystals.

"It's oxalic acid, a disinfectant," he said, "but it can be used instead of vinegar. I don't have any vinegar crystals. I've run out of soy paste too, there's just this *tiny* bit."

"It'll do," I said.

Tall Balls put his box on my bed and opened it: inside was a chess set made out of ebony, the pieces gleaming with a dark sheen. The characters on each piece were carved with a knife, each stroke made very carefully in seal script inlaid with gold and silver wire. It looked like a genuine antique. The chessboard was made of silk, and the words in the middle strip, "Chu River Han Boundary," were also written in seal characters. Everyone crowded around to see, to Tall Balls' immense satisfaction.

"It's an antique," he said, "from the Ming dynasty. It's very valuable. My father gave it to me when I left. Playing chess with you neophytes doesn't call for such a nice set. But today, with Wang Yisheng here, we're going to have a *proper* game."

Wang Yisheng, who had probably never seen such a fine chess set before, fondled the pieces carefully. Again, his face lit up and he rubbed his hands.

I poured boiling water on the soy paste and oxalic crystals and threw in the chopped onion, ginger, and garlic.

"Come and eat!"

There was a great clatter as everyone helped themselves to rice. Then we stretched out our chopsticks, tore off the snake meat, and dipped it into the seasoning, cries of admiration rising among the first mouthfuls.

I asked Wang Yisheng if he thought it tasted a little like crab.

"Don't know," Wang Yisheng replied with his mouth full. "Never eaten crab."

Tall Balls leaned forward. "You've never eaten crab?" he asked. "How can that be?"

Wang Yisheng didn't reply but concentrated on eating.

Tall Balls put down his bowl and chopsticks. "For the Mid-

Autumn Festival every year, my father invites a few distinguished guests home for crab, chess, wine-tasting, and poetry writing. They are all *very* cultivated people, and write *excellent* poems, which they inscribe on fans for each other. In a few years those fans will be *very* valuable, you know."

No one paid any attention to him but concentrated on the food. Seeing that the snake meat was disappearing, Tall Balls stopped talking and snatched up his chopsticks.

The meat was soon finished, leaving only two snake skeletons in the bowl. I carried over the steamed eggplant, mixing in a little garlic and salt. Then I poured out the hot water in the pot, added fresh water, put in the snake bones, and boiled it for soup. Everyone paused for a breather before extending their chopsticks again and quickly finishing the eggplant. Next I brought in the soup. The snake bones had separated as the water boiled and rattled around the bottom of the pot. I also added a few stems of wild fennel that I had picked near the huts. An unusual odor immediately filled our nostrils. We took turns ladling the snake-bone soup into our now empty rice bowls, swallowing it in small sips while it was hot. As we were no longer ravenous, we started to chat.

"Super, super," said Tall Balls, pushing his fingers through his hair. He pulled out a cigarette, offering it to Wang Yisheng, then put one in his own mouth. As he was putting the packet back in his pocket, he reconsidered and left it on the low table where we had been eating.

"What we've just had is called 'mountain treasure,'" he said with a flourish. "Seafood's beyond our reach. We often eat seafood at home—we're *most* particular about it. According to my father, my grandfather employed an old woman *exclusively* to spend the *whole* day picking out the bits of filth from the nests of cliff swallows. These nests are made of small fish and shrimp carried by the sea swallows in their beaks and stuck together with their saliva. So there's a *lot* of filthy matter inside, and they have to be cleaned *very* carefully, bit by bit—it takes a whole day to

A H   C H E N G

clean one, then you have to steam it slowly over a low flame. It's *extremely* good for your health to eat a little every day."

Wang Yisheng gaped. "One person spends all day doing nothing but fussing with bird nests? Son of a bitch! You could go and buy some fish and shrimp yourself and stew them up together—wouldn't that be just as good?"

Tall Balls gave a slight smile. "If it were, would the bird nests be so dear? In the first place, these nests are formed on cliffs overlooking the sea—people risk their *lives* to get them. In the second place, sea bird saliva is *very* valuable stuff—it's a heating tonic. Hence, there's risk of life and a great deal of time and trouble is spent. Being able to eat the nests also shows that the family is rich and has a certain social position."

Everyone agreed that bird's nest soup must be extremely tasty.

Tall Balls gave another slight smile. "I've tasted it—it *stinks*."

We all breathed a heavy sigh, now agreeing that it was hardly worth spending so much money on a mouthful of stinking soup.

Night deepened; the moon rising in the sky grew brighter. I lit the paraffin lamp, the flame instantly casting our shadows onto the walls.

"Shall we have a game, Wang Yisheng?" Tall Balls asked.

Wang Yisheng, who looked as if he had not yet recovered from the bird's nests, just nodded when he heard the question. Tall Balls went out.

"Eh?" exclaimed Wang Yisheng, surprised.

We laughed but no one offered an explanation.

After a while Tall Balls came back, dressed very smartly. There was a crowd of people behind him who wanted to get a glimpse of Wang Yisheng. Tall Balls slowly set out the board.

"Will you go first?" he asked.

"No, you go first," Wang Yisheng replied.

Everyone gathered around to watch, some sitting and some standing.

After about a dozen moves, Wang Yisheng looked a bit restless, kneading his hands discreetly. After about thirty moves, he said quickly, "Let's set them up again."

Surprised, we looked first at Wang Yisheng and then at Tall Balls, not knowing who was the winner.

Tall Balls gave a slight smile. "One win doesn't mean victory." He stretched out his hand, took a cigarette, and lit it.

Not displaying any emotion, Wang Yisheng silently set up the pieces again. The two made their moves again. After another dozen or so moves, Tall Balls sat still for a while. He finished his cigarette and they made a few more moves. Then Tall Balls said slowly, "Another round."

Everyone was taken by surprise again; some asked out loud who the winner was.

Wang Yisheng quickly raked the pieces into a pile, looked at Tall Balls and asked, "Play blind?" Muttering something under his breath, Tall Balls nodded his head.

The two of them proceeded to call out their moves. Several of us started to rub our heads and necks, saying it was not much fun when people played so well, not letting us know who was ahead. A few left, making the lamp flicker as they went out.

I felt a little chilly and asked Wang Yisheng if he wanted to get dressed. He didn't say anything. Feeling bored, I sat on the bed and watched the others as they looked from Tall Balls to Wang Yisheng—they could have been looking at a couple of ghosts. In the lamplight, Wang Yisheng sat hugging his knees, two deep hollows behind his collarbone. He was staring at the lamp and from time to time slapped at a mosquito landing on his body. Tall Balls' long legs were propped up against his chest, one large hand screening his face while he rapidly kneaded his fingers on the other hand. After they called their moves for a long time, Tall Balls dropped his hands and gave a quick smile.

"I've lost track, I can't remember *where* I am," he said, and set out the pieces on the board. Lifting his head, he looked at Wang Yisheng.

A H   C H E N G

"The world is yours," he said, and drew out a cigarette for his opponent. "*Who* did you learn your chess from?"

"From the world," replied Wang Yisheng, looking at Tall Balls.

"Super, super. You play a *super* game."

Realizing who was the winner, we gazed at Wang Yisheng, feeling pleased and relieved.

Tall Balls rubbed his hands together. "We don't have anyone here who can really play chess, so my game's gotten rusty. I'm so pleased to have run into you today—let's be friends."

"If I get a chance I'll certainly visit your father," Wang Yisheng said.

"Fine, excellent, *do* by all means go and see him if you have the chance. I'm but a dabbler." After a pause he added, "You'd have no trouble getting into the district tournament."

"What tournament?" Wang Yisheng asked.

"Our district's holding a sports day; there's going to be various kinds of games. I know the Secretary for Culture and Education, he used to live in our city and knows my father. When I came to the farm my father gave me a letter for him asking him to look after me. When I called on him, he suggested I play basketball. How could *I* play basketball? It's a *dreadfully* rough game, one's sure to get hurt. He sent me a letter about the sports day, telling me to try to get on the farm's board games team and take part in the district tournament—if I won, naturally it would be easy to get a transfer. With a game like yours, you'd have no trouble getting on the farm team. All you have to do is put your name down when you return to your branch. They're sure to let you in when they have the preliminaries at headquarters."

Wang Yisheng was very pleased. He got up and put on his clothes on, which made him look even thinner. We continued to talk into the night.

Toward midnight some of us started to wander off, leaving only the four in my hut plus Wang Yisheng and Tall Balls. Tall Balls stood up and said, "I'm going to fetch something to eat."

We waited expectantly. Within a few minutes he was back, stooping as he entered. He put the things on the bed: six small knobs of chocolate, half a packet of malt powder, and a cattie of fancy grade noodles wrapped in paper. We swallowed the chocolates in one gulp, licking our lips. The powder mixed with boiling water made six very weak bowls of malt drink, which we slurped down with a flourish.

"Is there anything else on earth like this, with this bitter-sweet flavor?" Wang Yisheng asked with a happy giggle.

I built up the fire again, put the pot on to boil, and dropped the noodles in. "Too bad we don't have any seasoning. "

"I still have some soy paste," Tall Balls said.

"Didn't you just have that tiny piece left?"

"Well, today's a special occasion, Wang Yisheng's here," Tall Balls said with some embarrassment. "I'll contribute a bit more." And he went off to get it.

After we finished eating, we each lit a smoke. Yawning, one of us said that we never thought Tall Balls would still have so much paste stashed away, so well hidden. Tall Balls said hastily in self-defense that this was really all he had left. We scoffed and said we'd go over and take a peek.

"That's enough," Wang Yisheng said. "What's his is his. To have stored such things for so long shows he knows how to get by. Tell me, Ni Bin, when does this tournament start?"

"It's at least six months away."

Wang Yisheng said no more.

"All right, time for bed," I said. "Wang Yisheng, you can sleep on my bed. Tall Balls, we can talk some more tomorrow."

We all started to make up the beds and arrange the mosquito nets. Wang Yisheng and I saw Tall Balls to the door, watching his long figure disappear in the bluish-white moonlight.

Wang Yisheng sighed. "Ni Bin's a good man," he said.

⌘

Wang Yisheng stayed one more day but insisted on leaving the morning after that. Tall Balls came to see him off, wearing his old work clothes and carrying his mattock over his shoulder. As the two shook hands, Ni Bin said, "We'll meet again in due course." Everyone waved goodbye to him from the distant mountainside. I accompanied him to the end of the ravine, then Wang Yisheng stopped me, saying, "You should go back now."

I gave him strict instructions that if he got into any trouble at the other branch farms he should send someone to tell me, and that if he passed by on his travels to drop in and spend a few days with us. Wang Yisheng straightened the strap of his bag and hurried down the road, his feet raising a fine dust, his shirt swaying from side to side, and his pants flapping as if he had no bottom.

III

After Wang's visit, whenever we had nothing to do we would often talked about him, recalling with great relish his bare-chested battle with Tall Balls. One day I told the others about the various hardships of his past and Tall Balls remarked, "My father used to say, 'Humble homes hatch heroes.' According to him, we are descendants of Ni Yunlin of the Yuan dynasty. This ancestor of ours was *very* fastidious, and of course he could afford to be finicky in the beginning when the family had money. Later there was a rebellion and the family was ruined, so Ni Yunlin sold the family property and took to the open road. Lodging at various remote backwater country inns, he often met *distinguished* scholars. On one occasion he got to know a rustic who could play chess, and learned from him how to play like an expert. Nowadays people only know that Ni Yunlin was one of the Four Yuan Masters, celebrated for his poetry, painting, and calligraphy, but *not* for his chess skills. When he became a Chan Buddhist later in his life, he brought chess into the Chan tradition; he created his own school, which has been handed down *only* within the family. Now that

Wang Yisheng's beaten me, whatever school he belongs to, he is an *expert* player."

None of us had ever heard of Ni Yunlin, and listening to Tall Balls' boasting we only believed half of what he said. But we accepted the fact that Tall Balls was no ordinary player, and as Wang Yisheng beat him, then Wang Yisheng must be even more sensational. The Educated Youths here were all from simple families, most of them quite poor, and naturally they thought even more highly of Wang Yisheng.

Almost six months passed with no further sign of Wang. We only heard reports from here and there of one called Wang Yisheng, nicknamed Chess Fool, who had played chess at such-and-such a place with so-and-so and had beaten him. We'd all be very pleased, and even when there was news of his defeat there'd be a chorus of denials from us: how could Wang Yisheng be defeated? I wrote a letter to him at his branch farm but received no reply. Everyone urged me to visit. But with so much going on, not least the fact that the Educated Youths in the state farm were always feuding, even taking potshots at each other with the firearms they had smuggled in, it was too dangerous on the road and I ended up not going.

One day up on the mountain Tall Balls took me aside to talk. He had put down his name for the tournament and would leave for farm headquarters in a couple of days. He asked me if I had heard any news of Wang Yisheng. I told him I hadn't. Everyone was certain that Wang Yisheng would turn up at the games so we agreed that we'd all ask for leave to go and watch.

A couple of days later, as work slackened off, everyone found various excuses to ask for leave in the hope of seeing Wang Yisheng. I was also given leave to go.

State farm headquarters was located in the district town, which we reached after two days on foot. Although a district township ranked immediately below the provincial capital in terms of local government, the town consisted of only two intersecting streets with a handful of shops, and the shelves were either empty or stocked with "Goods for Display Only: Not for Sale." Nonetheless, we were very excited, feeling that we had reached a thriving metropolis. We ate our way up and down the two streets, one restaurant after another, ordering only plain boiled pork, gorging ourselves on plate after plate of it. When we exited the last restaurant, patting our bellies, the sunlight dazzled our eyes and we were actually a bit drunk from so much meat. We found a grassy spot to lie down and have a smoke, dozing off one by one.

When we woke up, we walked back into town and cautiously ate only noodles. Then we set out for farm headquarters.

We marched over in high spirits, found the official in charge of culture and sports, and asked if anyone by the name of Wang Yisheng had registered. After spending forever scanning the register, the official said no. We didn't believe him and pulled over the register, pushing and shoving to look, but it was true. We asked the official if he could have been left off by mistake. He replied that the register had been compiled from the names submitted from each of the branch farms, that each person had been given a number and put into a group, and that the games would commence the next day. We gazed at each other, wondering what could have happened.

"Let's go and find Tall Balls," I said.

Tall Balls was in one of the huts for the participants. As soon as we saw him we questioned him.

"I was wondering, too," he said. "It's a complete *shambles* here. My number's for the board games, but they put me in with the *ball* games, and told me to take part in the headquarters team practice this evening. I argued with them for *hours* but it was no use, they said they were *depending* on me to put the ball in the net."

We started laughing.

"It doesn't matter what game you play, your food rations are better than average. But it's strange Wang Yisheng isn't here."

There was no sign of Wang Yisheng even after the games got underway. When we asked some people from his branch farm, they said they hadn't seen him for ages. We were worried but there was nothing we could do about it, so we went to watch Tall Balls play basketball.

Tall Balls was thoroughly miserable. He was completely ignorant of the rules; he couldn't catch the ball, and whenever he threw it he missed the hoop, the net, and even the board. Whenever the game became a little rough, he would withdraw and gaze wide-eyed at the rest of the players struggling over the ball. The culture and sports clerk tugged at his ears and scratched his jaw in irritation, while the audience rocked with laughter. At the end of each game, Tall Balls would loudly complain that it was a *barbaric* and *filthy* sport.

The two days of preliminaries ended and headquarters picked teams in each division to compete in the district games. Seeing that there was still no sign of Wang Yisheng, we all agreed to go back. Tall Balls decided to stay with the District Secretary for Culture and Education for another day or two, and saw us off a little way down the street. We had almost reached the end of the street when suddenly someone pointed: "Isn't that Wang Yisheng?"

We all recognized him at once. He was hurrying along the other side of the street oblivious to us. We yelled out his name. He stopped abruptly, looked over, and came running toward us across the street. Relieved to see him, I asked why he wasn't competing in the games.

"I've taken so much leave these last six months to play chess," he said with a harried look, "that when it came time to register they said I hadn't been pulling my weight and refused. I've only just now been able to escape. What's happening? How are the chess matches going?"

Speaking at once, we told him that the preliminaries were over and now the local teams were competing for the district championship. Wang Yisheng was quiet for a moment, then said, "Oh well, at least I can see the top local players compete for the district championship. That should be worth watching."

"Haven't you eaten yet?" I asked. "Come on, we can grab something in town."

Tall Balls felt very sorry for Wang Yisheng and shook hands with him. We crowded into a small restaurant and ordered a meal, sighing with each mouthful.

"I'm staying to watch the rest of the chess tournament," Wang Yisheng said. "How about the rest of you? Do you have to get back?"

The others said they'd already been away too long and had to be getting back.

"I'll stay on for another couple of days to keep you company," I said. "Tall Balls will be here, too."

A few others agreed to hang around as well.

Tall Balls took us to visit the Secretary for Culture and Education, to see if there was any chance of getting Wang Yisheng into the tournament. It didn't take long to get there. The low iron gate in front of the building was locked, and when we asked to enter, the guard asked us who we were looking for. Then he recognized Tall Balls and shut up, gesturing for us to wait.

Eventually we were led into a large room. The first thing that struck me was a row of freshly watered plants on the windowsill. On one huge wall hung a single scroll with a poem by Chairman Mao mounted on pale yellow silk. The only furniture in the room was a few cane chairs and a tea table covered with newspapers and mimeographed reports. A moment later the Secretary emerged, a big fat man who quickly shook each of us by the hand, called for someone to clear off the table, and invited us to sit. Besides Tall Balls, no one had ever been in the home of someone of his rank, and we each glanced around to take it all in.

The Secretary settled in and asked, "Are you all Ni Bin's school-mates?"

We looked at each other, not sure who should answer.

Tall Balls leaned forward. "They're all from my work unit. This is Wang Yisheng." As he spoke he waved his hand toward Wang.

The Secretary looked at him. "Ah, so you're Wang Yisheng? Good. Ni Bin's mentioned you frequently the past few days. How's it going? Have you been chosen for the district tournament?"

Wang Yisheng was about to answer when Tall Balls quickly interrupted.

"Wang Yisheng was held up by some business and couldn't put his name down. Now that he's sorted things out, could he possibly enter the district tournament? What do you think?"

The Secretary lightly patted the arms of his chair with his pudgy hands for a minute, then slowly rubbed the groove below his nose with his middle finger.

"So that's how it is. Unfortunately, it's not that simple. If you haven't qualified in the preliminaries it's not that simple. I've heard you're a real genius, but if you compete without having qualified, people will talk, won't they?"

Wang Yisheng lowered his head. "I don't really have to compete. I'd just like to watch."

"That's no problem," the Secretary said. "You're welcome to come and watch. Ni Bin, go over to that desk, the one on the left, there's a printed timetable for the games. Bring it here and let's have a look and see how the chess tournament's organized."

Tall Balls hurried into the inner room and returned with the papers, glancing over them. "The tournament goes on for *three* days!" he shouted, and handed the pages over to the Secretary.

The Secretary didn't even bother to look, tossing the timetable onto the tea table and lightly clapping his palms.

"Yes, there are several teams aren't there? Well, now? Any other problems?"

We stood up, thanking him and saying we'd be off. The Secretary shook hands very quickly with the person nearest him. "Ni Bin, you're coming around this evening, eh?"

Ni Bin accepted with a bow and left with the rest of us. Reaching the street, we breathed a sigh of relief and burst out talking and joking.

We wandered down the street, discussing how we could stay for another three nights since we didn't have enough money to last that long. Wang Yisheng said that not lodging at an inn would save a large amount, and that he could find us another place to sleep despite our numbers. With some embarrassment Ni Bin said he could stay in the Secretary's house. Together, we set off to search for lodging for the rest of us.

It turned out that Wang Yisheng had already visited the town and knew a painter in the Cultural Center, so he hauled us along to see if we might crash there. As we entered the Center, we could hear people singing and playing instruments and guessed it was the propaganda team rehearsing. We saw three or four girls wearing blue cotton knit jumpers and slacks. They walked toward us swinging their hips, chests thrust out. They swept through us, looking straight ahead, making no attempt to walk around. We hastily stepped aside, blushing a little.

"They're the district's star performers," said Tall Balls in a whisper. "It's *ever* so hard to find their sort of talent in such a small district."

We turned around to gape again at the star performers.

The painter lived in a corner of the building beside a small courtyard, hens and ducks wandering in and out of the doorway. Random stacks of junk overgrown with grass had been thrown along the foot of the wall. The door itself was hidden behind a mass of clothes and sheets hung up to dry. Leading us bent down through the washing, Wang Yisheng called out the painter's name. We heard things banging and crashing as someone came out.

"Oh, it's you!" said the painter, seeing Wang Yisheng. "Come in, all of you."

The painter's quarters was a tiny room with a small wooden bed; books, magazines, tubes of paint, paper, and brushes were splayed around, and his paintings were pinned across every inch of the walls. As we filed in, the painter shifted things around to make room. We sat down squeezed together, not daring to move. The painter made his way past us and returned with a thermos. He poured hot water for each of us as we passed around an assortment of mugs and bowls.

The painter sat down with us to drink. "Are you also taking part in the competition?" he asked Wang Yisheng.

With a sigh, Wang Yisheng told him the situation.

"Then there's nothing that can be done," the painter said. "How long do you need to stay?"

"That's what I wanted to see you about," Wang Yisheng said. "These are all friends of mine. Do you think you could find somewhere for us to crash for a couple nights?"

The painter muttered under his breath. "You've always squeezed in here comfortably enough, whenever you've shown up. With this many, though, hmmm … let me see …"

Suddenly his eyes brightened. "There's an auditorium in the Cultural Center and the stage is actually quite big. Tonight there's a performance for those taking part in the games, but you can sleep on the stage when it's over. How about that? And I can get you all in to see the show. The electrician's a friend of mine; I can ask him and there shouldn't be any problems about you sleeping there. It'll be a bit dirty, though."

We assured him we couldn't be happier. Looking relieved, Tall Balls stood up carefully. "Well then, gentlemen, I'll be on my way."

We tried to stand up to say goodbye but none of us could get to our feet. He pushed us down, telling us repeatedly to sit, and then in one stride he was outside.

"What a beanpole!" the painter said. "Does he play basketball?"

　　　　　　　　　　　　　　　　　　　　　A H C H E N G

We burst out laughing and told him about Tall Balls and basketball.

The painter replied, "Yes, you look pretty miserable yourselves. Come on, let's get you cleaned up. I'll come with you."

We filed out, one by one, but still couldn't help banging into things.

It turned out that there was a river some distance outside town, and it took us a long time to get there on foot. The river was not particularly broad but the current was very fast, small eddies swirling near the bank.

With no one else around we stripped down and washed thoroughly, using up the piece of soap the painter had brought with him. We also soaked our clothes in the river, pounded them with stones, wrung them out, and spread them on some rocks to dry. Apart from a few swimmers, the rest of us stretched out on the bank to sunbathe.

The painter, who had finished washing before us, was sitting to the side, sketching in a notebook. When I noticed this, I went over and stood beside him, looking over his shoulder. It turned out that he was sketching us in the nude. From his drawings I discovered that we boys actually looked remarkably strong, given our hard work up in the mountains every day. I couldn't repress a sigh of admiration. The others also gathered around to look, their bottoms flashing white.

"People who do manual labor," the painter said, "have very distinctive, clean lines to their muscles. Each part may not have developed completely balanced, but that's the way with real bodies, the endless variations. When I did life studies at the academy, we mostly drew female models in standard poses. Even the male models were always stationary, and I couldn't get a feeling for their muscles in motion. The more I painted the stiffer the bodies looked. Today's a rare opportunity."

One of us said that genitalia weren't nice to look at so the painter blotted out the boy's penis with his pencil, turning it into a blob. We burst out laughing. By then our clothes had dried and we got dressed.

It was now close to dusk. The sun was suspended between two mountains, turning the ripples along the river to gold and the rocks on the banks to red-hot iron. Birds skimmed to and fro across the water, their cries reaching us from far away. On the opposite bank someone was bellowing a folksong, drawing out each note; we couldn't see him, but we could follow his voice as it slowly faded away. We gazed after him, transfixed. A long silence passed. Wang Yisheng sighed, not saying anything. We started the long walk back.

Once in town we dragged the painter along to eat with us. He certainly knew how to drink. It was dark by now and the painter brought us to the stage door at the back of the auditorium. He nodded to someone and said a few words. Then he instructed us to enter very quietly and crouch in the wings to watch.

The starting time came and went without the curtains opening. Wang said it was because the Secretary had not arrived yet. The performers, in costume and make-up, were pacing up and down backstage, limbering up and joking with each other. Suddenly there was a stir and when I lifted the curtain to peek, I saw the Secretary stroll in and sit down in the front row. The seats around him were empty, but the rest of the auditorium was densely packed.

The performance began. The actors overflowed with so much energy that dust rose around them. Onstage, their eyes shone with tears, but as soon as they retired to the wings they laughed and joked about everything that had gone wrong. Wang Yisheng was totally transported, his face alternately sunny and overcast, his mouth wide in wonder. There was no trace of the composure he displayed before a chessboard. When the show ended, he started clapping alone from the wings. I hastily stopped him and looked out beyond the stage. The Secretary had already gone, who

AH CHENG

knows when, and the two front rows were still empty.

We emerged and groped our way through the dark to the painter's home. Tall Balls was already inside. When he saw us coming, he and the painter met us outside.

"Wang Yisheng, you *can* take part in the tournament!" the painter said.

"How can that be?" asked Wang Yisheng.

Tall Balls said that when he was at the Secretary's this evening the Secretary had begun to chat. He said that a dozen or so years ago he had often visited Tall Balls' home and had seen a number of paintings there. He wondered whether they had been lost since the Movement started. Tall Balls said that they still had a few left, at which the Secretary fell silent. He then went on to say that it shouldn't be any problem getting Tall Balls transferred—he could find a place for him in the District Office for Culture and Education; one word with his subordinates and it would be settled quickly. He suggested that Tall Balls write home and tell his family. He then returned to the subject of paintings and antiques, saying that nowadays no one knew how valuable these things were, but that he himself was very concerned about them. Tall Balls volunteered to write a letter home to see if his family could send the Secretary one or two scrolls. As the Secretary has been such a great help, it was only right to show some gratitude. He added that back on the farm he had an ebony chess set dating from the Ming, a very fine piece of craftsmanship, and if the Secretary fancied it he could bring it along next time. The Secretary was very pleased and urged Tall Balls to do so. He then added that he could have a word with his subordinates about our friend Wang Yisheng, that there was no need to be so strict in what was only a district competition, and one shouldn't discriminate against personal friends at the expense of recognizing talent. He picked up the phone and indeed there'd be no problem, the Secretary was not to worry, Wang Yisheng could take part in the tournament the next day.

We are all very pleased to hear this and praised Tall Balls for his crude tactics. Wang Yisheng, however, said nothing. After Tall Balls left, the painter took us to look for the electrician, who opened the back door to the auditorium and let us sneak in. The electrician noticed that it had turned cool and asked if we'd like to take down the curtains to use as blankets. A good idea, we said, and proceeded to get in each others' way as we climbed up, un-hooked the curtains, and spread them on the stage. One of us walked to the front of the stage, bowed to the empty seats, and announced in the shrill tones of an MC, "The next item on the program is ... sleep. Ladies and gentlemen, may I present ..."

Chuckling at this we crawled under the curtains and lay down.

I had been lying there for a while when I realized that Wang Yisheng wasn't asleep either.

"Go to sleep," I said, "you're playing in the tournament tomor-row!"

"No," said Wang Yisheng in the darkness. "I'm not interested. Ni Bin means well, but I don't want to enter the tournament."

"What's the matter!" I said. "You get to play in the tournament, Tall Balls gets his transfer. Why bother about a chess set?"

"It's his father's set!" Wang Yisheng said. "It's not a matter of whether it's valuable or not—it's a family treasure. The blank chess set that ma left me, I've always guarded it with my life. Even if it's not too hard now to earn a living, I can't forget what she told me. How can Ni Bin give it away?"

"Tall Balls' family has money," I said. "A chess set's nothing to them. They'd be glad to part with it if they thought their son could be a bit more comfortable."

"Anyway, I'm not going to play in the tournament as part of a deal; it would look as if I was pulling strings. Whether I win or not when I play is up to me, but if I entered the tournament like this there'd be a lot of spiteful gossip."

Another who hadn't fallen asleep must have heard and mut-tered, "Fool!"

Early the next morning we awoke covered in dirt. We found some water and wiped ourselves off, then invited the painter to join us for a meal. He put up a determined protest, and as we were talking Tall Balls arrived, looking very cheerful.

"I'm not going to take part in the tournament," Wang Yisheng said to him.

Everyone gaped.

"Terrific! What do you mean you won't take part?" Tall Balls asked. "There's going to be people from the provincial capital in the audience!"

"I'm not taking part and that's all there is to it."

I explained the situation and Tall Balls sighed.

"The Secretary's a man of culture, he's *frightfully* keen on these things. The chess set is a family heirloom, but I really can't bear living on a state farm any longer. I just want to live anywhere that's clean, and not get filthy every day. You can't eat a chess set— it's worth giving away if it'll smooth things out for me. My family's been going through a rough time, too, they won't blame me."

The painter folded his arms in front of his chest, then lifted a hand to rub his face. "No one would blame you, Ni Bin," he said, looking up at the sky. "You're not asking for anything special. I've also done stupid things these past couple of years. Life's become a little too down-to-earth. Fortunately I can still paint. How may one abolish care? Only by ... ah, well."

Wang Yisheng looked at the painter in astonishment. He turned slowly to face Tall Balls. "Thanks, Ni Bin. When the tournament decides the top players, I'll ask each one for a game. But I won't take part in the tournament."

All of a sudden Tall Balls became very animated and clenched his fists.

"That's it!" he said. "Why don't I have a word with the Secretary; we'll organize a *friendly*. If you win this match, it's beyond question you're the *true* winner. And if you lose, it won't be too much of a letdown."

Wang Yisheng stared at him. "Whatever you do don't talk to any Secretary. I'll talk to the winners myself. If they're willing, I'll play the top three together at the same time."

There was nothing the rest of us could say so we went to watch the different competitions. It was a fun time. Wang Yisheng made a beeline for the chess arena and monitored the display boards outside that showed the results of play for each game. The top three players were decided the following day. After the last match the prize-giving and performance ended the festivities. It was so noisy around the viewing stand that it was impossible to hear who got which prize.

Tall Balls told us to wait. Minutes later he brought over two men wearing cadre uniforms. Tall Balls did the introductions: they were numbers two and three respectively in the championship.

"This is Wang Yisheng," Tall Balls said. "He plays a superb game. He'd like to play with you two masters—it's a chance for all of you to *learn from each other.*"

The two men looked at Wang Yisheng. "Why didn't you take part in the tournament?" they asked. "We've been stuck here several days already, we have to get back."

"I don't want to hold you up," Wang Yisheng said. "I'll play against the two of you at once."

They glanced at each other in understanding.

"Blind chess?"

Wang Yisheng nodded.

The two immediately changed their attitude and smiled. "We've never played blind chess before."

"Don't worry, you can follow along on the display boards. Come on, let's find a place."

Word spread quickly. People from different parts of the district were saying that a boy from the state farm who hadn't taken part in the tournament was challenging the decision and wanted to take on the number two and three players, both of them at once. A swarm of people gathered around us, pushing and shoving to look. Feeling responsible for Wang Yisheng we took up positions at his side.

Wang Yisheng lowered his head. "Let's go," he said to the other two. "We're too conspicuous here."

Someone pushed his way forward and said, "Who's looking for a game? Is it you? My uncle's the champion; he heard that you're challenging the result and told me to invite you over."

"It's not necessary," Wang Yisheng said slowly. "If your uncle is willing, I'll take on the three of you together."

This caused a sensation, and together we pushed our way toward the arena. When we reached the street, the large crowd followed us. People walking by saw us and asked what was happening, wondering whether the Educated Youths were fighting. When they found out what it was all about, they joined in too.

By the time we were halfway down the street, there must have been nearly a thousand people milling around us. Even the shop assistants and their customers came out to see the commotion. The long-distance bus couldn't get through, and when the passengers stuck their heads out the window, they could see the whole street brimming with heads bobbing up and down, dust flying, and paper scraps being trodden underfoot.

A crackpot was standing woodenly in the middle of the street, singing tunelessly. Someone was merciful enough to pull him aside, and he continued his song propped up against a wall. Four or five dogs dashed in and out, barking noisily as if they were leading a wolf hunt.

There were easily a few thousand people around us when we reached the arena, kicking up large clouds of dust that took ages to settle. The slogans and signs of the competition had already been dismantled. A man came out, paling at the sight of so many people. Tall Balls went over to negotiate with him. Gazing at the crowd, the man nodded his head several times in rapid succession until he finally understood that we wanted to use the chess hall and hastily opened the door, repeating, "Yes of course, yes of course." When he saw that the whole crowd wanted to get in, he bristled in alarm. A few of us immediately stood guard at the entrance, letting in only Tall Balls, Wang Yisheng, and the two prize-winners.

At this point another man walked up and said to us, "If this master player is willing to play against three, he won't mind adding one more—why not me, too?"

This created another sensation, and more people put their names forward. I wasn't sure what to do and went inside to tell Wang Yisheng.

Wang Yisheng bit his lip. "What do you two think?" he asked the other two.

They jumped up and assured him that they had no objection.

I went outside to count. Including the champion there'd be ten opponents altogether.

"Ten is inauspicious," said Tall Balls. "*Nine* would be better."

And so only six were added to the three.

The champion had still not put in an appearance, but someone arrived to report that since they were playing blind chess, the champion would stay at home and send a messenger to pass on his moves. Wang Yisheng thought it over and agreed. The nine left were then shut inside the hall.

The board on the wall outside wasn't big enough, so eight full-sized sheets of white paper were marked into squares. Then someone cut out square, cardboard chess pieces, wrote their positions in red and black, pasted a loop of string on the back, and hung them on the nails at the intersections of the lines. As the pieces fluttered in the breeze, a murmur of excitement passed through the crowd in the street.

More and more people arrived. The latecomers tried to push their way to the front, but failing to get through, they grabbed hold of anyone and asked if it was another notice about executions. Women carrying children formed a distant outer circle.

Many had parked their bicycles and stood on the rear rack, craning forward to see, though every time the crowd surged they'd fall over and another round of shouting would follow. Older children burrowed in and out, propelled between the legs of the adults. The din created by these thousands caused the street to resonate with a sound like muffled thunder.

Wang Yisheng was sitting on a chair in the middle of the hall, his hands on his knees, staring blankly ahead. His face was covered in dust, giving him the air of a criminal brought in for interrogation. I couldn't help smiling as I crossed over to dust him off a little. He pressed my hand and I could feel him trembling slightly.

"It's gotten out of control," he said in a low voice. "You and your friends keep an eye out, if there's any trouble we'll make a break for it."

"There won't be," I said. "As long as you win everything will work out. Show them what you've got. What's the matter? Are you feeling confident? Nine people! Including the top three!"

Wang Yisheng muttered something under his breath. "It's not the gentlemen," he said, "it's the barbarians that scare me. The people who participated in the tournament—I've seen how they play; but one of the other six may prove to be my downfall. Here, take my bag, and don't lose it whatever happens. It's got ..." Wang Yisheng looked at me. "Ma's blank chess set."

His thin face was parched and grimy; even the depression below his nose was black, his hair was sticking straight in the air, his throat was working, and his eyes were terribly dark. I knew he was pushing himself to the limit and felt rather anxious, but I just said, "Take care!" and left. He was alone in the middle of the hall, looking at no one, as inert as a lump of iron.

The game got under way. Not another sound rose from the thousands of onlookers. A volunteer shouted out the chess moves, his short staccato yelps followed by long pauses. Another volunteer outside moved the chess pieces. The eight sheets of paper rustled in the breeze with the fluttering pieces. The sun cast its slanting rays over the crowd in a dazzling glare. The people in the first twenty or thirty rows sat on the ground, tilting their heads back to see, while the people toward the back formed densely packed rows of rough, local peasant faces, their hair tossing around in the wind. No one moved, as if their own lives were at stake.

Without warning an ancient recollection welled up inside me and my throat contracted. Books I had read appeared in a blur, some near, some far away. Xiang Yu and Liu Bang, who had always been my heroes, laughed at each other like idiots, while the dark-skinned soldiers whose corpses were strewn across the wilderness crawled up from underground, slowly, dumbly. A woodcutter raised his ax, singing a weird tune. Then all of a sudden I seemed to see the Fool's mother, her feeble hands folding page after page of a book.

I found myself reaching inside Wang Yisheng's bag. I groped about, then closed my fingers around a small bundle and drew it out. It was a small pouch made of old blue twill with a bat embroidered on it for luck. Each side was scalloped with very fine stitching. I took out one of the chess pieces, which was indeed tiny. In the sunlight it was translucent; like an eye, it stared at me tenderly. I clutched it in my hand.

The sun finally set and the air became cool and fresh. People were still watching but had started to converse with each other. Whenever the person inside called out a move by Wang Yisheng, a roar echoed outside. Several people were engaged as bicycle-riding messengers conveying the moves to the champion sitting at home. Things became less formal, jokes floated around.

I went inside again. One look at Tall Balls' evident glee and I knew I could relax. "How's it going?" I asked. "I can't follow what they're doing."

Tall Balls swept his fingers through his hair. "It's *fantastic*," he said, "*fantastic.* I've never seen such a line-up. Look for yourself, *nine* of them against him alone, *nine* interlocking games! One man taking on all challengers! I'm going to write to my father about it, I'll send him the full transcript."

At this point two men rose from their boards and gave Wang Yisheng a deep bow. "It's an honor to admit defeat before a master."

They walked out, kneading their fingers. Wang Yisheng gave a polite nod and glanced at their empty places.

Wang had not changed position. He sat with both hands on his knees, staring straight ahead as if gazing far away into the distance, while his eyes seemed to focus right in front of him. His dirt-stained shirt hung loosely over his thin shoulders. Finally, after an interminable interval, his Adam's apple moved.

For the first time I recognized that chess was also a physical activity, a marathon, a double marathon! At school, I had taken part in some long-distance running. For the initial stretch I'd feel quite exhausted, but after a certain point, my brain seemed to stop functioning, as if I were a plane without a pilot, or a hang glider at its peak who needs only to float down. But with chess you're involved in a battle of wits from start to finish, a battle to trap your opponent and force him to the wall without ever allowing yourself a moment's respite.

I felt a sudden pang of anxiety about Wang Yisheng's health. Over the last few days, what with cash being tight, we weren't able to eat well, and we also fell asleep late. None of us had imagined an occasion like this might arise.

As I watched Wang Yisheng sitting there like a rock, I felt a wave of indignation on his behalf: "Hold on!" I whispered. Carrying timber in the mountains, two people helped with each log, and whether or not the road was hardly a road, the trail hardly a trail, we still had to grit our teeth and not let go even if it killed us. If someone couldn't hold on and weakened, of course he'd get injured, but the other person would receive such a shock from the vibration at the other end of the log that he'd vomit blood. Here, though, Wang Yisheng had to cross the terrain by himself—there was no way we could help him.

I filled a bowl with cold water, sidled up to him quietly, and stood in front of his line of vision. He shivered and looked at me with eyes like knives. Eventually he recognized me and smiled dryly. I pointed to the bowl of water. He picked up the bowl and was about to drink when one of the players announced a move. He brought the bowl up to his lips, not a ripple appearing on the surface. He announced his counter-move with his gaze still on the rim of the bowl, then slowly raised it to his lips.

The next player announced a move. Wang fixed his mouth to the bowl's rim and, after a long pause, declared his and finally took a gulp of water. His swallow sounded horribly loud, and tears filled his eyes. As he passed the bowl back he gazed at me, inexpressible emotions simmering in his eyes. A drop of water slowly trickled down from the corner of his mouth, forming a runnel through the dirt on his chin and neck. I tried to pass the bowl back to him, but he held up his hand to stop me and returned into his world again.

It was already dark when I went outside again. Some of the locals had made torches out of pine branches; others were shining flashlights—beams of bright, circular, yellow light. The district offices must have finished work for the day, for there were even more people than before. Even the dogs squatting in front of the crowd were watching the chess moves with a mournful gaze, as if they shared in the general anxiety.

The two or three Educated Youths from our team were surrounded by people asking questions. Before long, remarks were being passed from mouth to mouth: "Wang Yisheng … Chess Fool … he's an Educated Youth … he plays Daoist chess." It sounded ridiculous, and I thought about wandering through the crowd to explain, but I stayed where I was—let them gossip! My spirits began to rise. By now there were only three active sheets remaining on the boards.

A shout rang out from the crowd; I turned around to look. There was only one game left, the one with the champion, and only a handful of pieces left on the board.

Wang Yisheng's black soldiers ranged throughout the enemy camp, with only the old general steadfastly on guard behind the lines, and an advisor accompanying him. It was like an emperor chatting with a favorite courtier as he waited for the army at the front to return in triumph to the court. You could almost make out the attendants lighting long red candles for the banquet, while others softly tuned their instruments, waiting for the messenger to kneel and report victory before the music blared forth.

My belly emitted a long rumble and my legs felt wobbly. I picked a spot and sat down, looking up at the last encirclement, afraid that something might go wrong.

The red pieces hadn't moved for ages and everyone was getting impatient. A buzz spread through the crowd as people looked to see if the messenger was on his way.

Suddenly there was a disturbance and the crowd began to make way. I caught sight of an old man with a bald head, shuffling forward on someone's arm. He scanned the final moves on the eight completed games, his mouth working silently.

It was the reigning district champion, the descendant of a distinguished local family who had "come down the mountain" to play a few games for the fun of it, not expecting to seize the crown. He had criticized the general level of play in the tournament, lamenting the decline in standards.

When the old man had finished looking at the sheets, he straightened his clothes, stamped his feet on the ground, lifted his head, and entered the hall, helped along by his supporter.

The crowd pressed forward.

I rushed in after them and watched as the old man stopped just inside the door to look ahead.

Wang Yisheng was sitting alone in the center of the arena, staring at us, his hands resting on his knees, apparently seeing nothing, hearing nothing—a slender iron rod. High above, an electric lamp cast a dim light on his face: his eyes were deeply sunken, as dark as if they had seen boundless worlds, an infinite universe. His life-force seemed to be concentrated in his wild hair, a force that didn't dissipate but seemed to gently spread, searing our faces.

The crowd fell still; no one uttered a word. Stories about the Chess Fool had been circulating for so long, and yet what sat before them was a small, thin, dark, motionless ghost. Gasps rose through the crowd.

The old man coughed from deep beneath his diaphragm, the sound reverberating loud and clear through the hall. Wang Yisheng suddenly retracted his gaze and noticed the crowd. He tried to stand up but couldn't move. The old man pushed aside the person holding him, took a few steps forward, halted, and rubbing his belly with clasped hands, began to speak in a strong, resonant voice.

"Young man, my age and infirmity have prevented me from attending this field of battle in person, obliging me to relay my moves by messenger. You are a mere child, yet you have a true understanding of chess. I have witnessed how you fuse the Dao-ist and Chan schools. Your intuitive grasp of strategy is remark-able. You seize the initiative with a show of strength, and rally your reserves once your opponent has attacked. You dispatch your dragon to rule the waves, and your force traverses Yin and Yang. The scholar-generals of past and present could do no more than this. I am most fortunate that in my declining years you have stepped forward to take my place. It is of no small moment to me that the art of chess has not wholly degenerated in China. I would hope that we may be friends despite the disparity in our years. Now that I have played thus far, I would prefer to regard it as a friendly game. I wonder if you would agree to a draw and not disgrace an old and feeble man?"

Wang Yisheng made another effort but still couldn't stand up. Tall Balls and I rushed over and lifted him up, supporting him under his arms. His legs were still crossed: they couldn't straighten out but dangled in mid-air. It felt as if I was holding only a few feathers of weight.

I motioned to Tall Balls to put him down and massage his legs. The audience pressed closer; the old man shook his head with a sigh. Tall Balls' large hands gently but vigorously massaged Wang Yisheng's body, face, and neck. Soon, Wang Yisheng went limp and he leaned back against us. Rasping noises came from his throat as he slowly opened his mouth, closed it, and opened it again.

After a long time, he managed to croak, "It's a draw."

Looking deeply moved, the old man said, "Would you like to come to my home this evening to rest? Perhaps spend one or two days recovering and we can talk about chess?"

Wang Yisheng shook his head. "No," he said softly, "I'm with friends. We came together and we'll stay together. We're going ... we're going to the Cultural Center ... I've got a friend there."

"Let's go back to my place," called the painter from within the crowd. "I've already bought some food, you can all come. What an event!"

The crowd slowly surged toward us as we went out, the torches blazing in a circle. Local people from the town and from the surrounding countryside gathered around us. Each tried to catch a glimpse of the King of Chess, his languid figure; each nodded and sighed.

I helped Wang Yisheng along, the lights following us the whole way. At last we entered the Cultural Center and headed for the painter's room. Although some were helping us disperse the crowd, there was still a mob pressing against the windows. This made the painter so nervous he hastily stashed away some of his paintings.

The people outside gradually left, but Wang Yisheng remained in a semi-stupor. I was suddenly aware that I was still clutching the piece from his chess set. I opened my hand to let him see it. Wang Yisheng gazed at it vacantly, not seeming to recognize it. Then a noise rumbled low in his throat. He retched and spat out globs of phlegm.

"Ma," he said, with a sob in his voice, "today, I ... ma ..."

We all felt very awkward. Between us we swept the floor, fetched some food and water, and tried to calm him down. When Wang stopped crying, the emotion that had been stifling him lifted and he began to recover his spirits. We all began to eat.

The painter ended up getting completely drunk, and, ignoring the rest of us, lay down on the bed and went to sleep. With the electrician showing the way and Tall Balls falling in behind, we trooped over to the auditorium and slipped under the curtain to sleep.

It was so dark you couldn't see the fingers on your hands. Wang Yisheng instantly fell fast asleep. I still seemed to hear the noise of the crowd beside me and see the torches blazing bright and the mountain folk, their faces like iron, walking through the forest carrying firewood and chanting rhythmically. I smiled, thinking that I could never have known this pleasure had I not become one of the common people myself. My home was gone, my family had been destroyed, and with cropped hair I carried a mattock day in and day out. And yet this in itself contained a true human life. Only now had I come to know real fortune and happiness. Food and shelter are basic needs, and since the dawn of the human race these two things have been our daily preoccupation. But to be limited by them does not amount to a true human existence.

Fatigue gradually overpowered me. Wrapping myself in the curtain, I fell into a deep sleep.

the
KING
of
CHILDREN

I

By 1976, I had been working in the countryside for seven years. I had learned how to clear the land, burn off the undergrowth, dig holes, transplant seedlings, hoe the fields, turn the soil, sow grain, feed the pigs, make mud bricks, and cut grass. If I was a little slower than the others it was only because I wasn't as strong. This didn't bother me, though, as after all I was still earning my keep.

One January day, the local Party Secretary summoned me over to his place. Not knowing what it was about, I squatted at the threshold of his door, waiting for him to speak. He tossed over a cigarette, but I didn't notice until it dropped on the floor. I quickly picked it up and looked up at him, grinning. He threw over some matches; I lit my cigarette and inhaled.

"Gold Sand River?" I asked.

He nodded, puffing at his water-pipe so that it burbled.

When he finished his smoke, he leaned the pipe against the wall, brushed the dust off his rough hands, blew his nose between his fingers, and asked, "Coping with our life here with the team?"

I looked up and nodded.

"You're a bright guy," he went on.

This alarmed me, and I wondered if he was being sarcastic. I turned his words over in my mind like a millstone, but as I hadn't done anything wrong, I smiled: "Are you kidding? If it's a job I can manage, give me the assignment and I'll do my best."

"You're out of my hands now. The branch farm has transferred you to teach in the school. You are to report for work tomorrow. Do a good job over there, don't let us down. My third son, you know, learning doesn't come easy to him. Try to encourage him a little now that you're at the school. If he acts up, punish him; just let me know and I'll punish him, too."

He passed over a sheet of paper. There it was, written in black and white with a big red seal at the bottom to verify it.

I left the Party Secretary's home in high spirits and returned to the hut to pack my bedding. Brownie was sitting cross-legged on his bed, picking a thorn from the sole of his foot. He paid no attention as I folded up my quilt and mattress but peered over when I started tying up my things with a string.

"What the hell are you doing?"

Keeping my voice steady, I casually described what happened.

Brownie leaped down to the floor and pulled on his pants. "Fuck you, you bastard! Why on earth would they let you go and teach?"

"How should I know? It's a notification from above, written in black and white. There can't be anyone else in our team with exactly the same name as me!"

Brownie shuffled on his shoes and walked out, brushing off his backside.

A few minutes later the whole gang appeared, grinning and cracking jokes. My luck had turned, they said, the hard times were over, what a cushy job teaching kids to read, whatever the weather I'd have a roof over my head, and so on. They called me a rotten little traitor, and insisted that I tell them what strings I had pulled to make the school payroll.

I told them that they need only go to the school to ask, and that if I had really been pulling strings I'd be a ... I was about to use the usual swear word we usually batted around but remembered I had better clean up my language if I was going to teach, so I just mumbled something indistinct.

They said nobody wanted to "institute an investigation," but that I shouldn't forget them after I left, and that whenever they passed the school on the way to a meeting or a movie they would stop over. I said of course.

"Leave your mattock and knife here with me," Brownie suggested. "You won't be needing them any more."

I wasn't happy about leaving these things behind and muttered, "Who says I won't be needing them? I've heard we must participate in manual labor there once a week."

"That kind of labor is just jerking off."

"You can keep the mattock but not the knife. If I need the mattock at school I'll come back for it."

Brownie wasn't too pleased but added, "You don't report until tomorrow, what's the point of packing today? You're that keen to leave? Stay another night and I'll go with you tomorrow."

I actually felt a bit foolish overdoing it like this, so I unrolled my bedding and slowly put my things back. The others still hung around chatting and joking. Someone said seriously that the fact I had completed four years of secondary school must have made a difference after all.

That night a few of my special pals cooked dinner, brought over some of the local maize liquor, and we celebrated. For a brief time I became someone whose name was on everyone's lips, as if I had been posted to the UN or landed on the moon. After a few drinks I got a bit sentimental.

"After I've gone I won't forget my friends, whatever it is you want of me. And when you get married and have kids of your own, they'll learn to read in my class—I won't let them down, either."

"Sure," they said.

Laidi, who cooked for our team, joined the party and found herself a seat. "I'm going to miss you *so much*," she said, casting a meaningful glance at me.

Others laughed, saying she was only getting emotional because I would be on the school payroll and that she was hoping to be transferred to the school as a cook.

Laidi parted her fat legs, put her hands on her hips, and tossed her head.

"Don't think that standing in front of a stove is all I'm good for!" she yelled. "I can sing, too, can't I, and I know how to read music! Why shouldn't I teach music at the school! Look into it for me, Beanpole, won't you? *You* know damn well I can teach. Just give me a score and I'll have the whole school singing within an hour!" (My friends called me Beanpole because I was so skinny.)

She poured herself a cup and raised it toward me. "If you do this for me I'll drink ten cups to your health." She threw back her head and drank without waiting for my reply.

"Eh? Whose liquor do you think you're drinking!" Brownie said.

Laidi didn't even blush. She banged down the cup and gave him a dirty look.

"What's so precious about this dog piss! You call yourselves men and you're not even halfway through the bottle yet! What woman would want to settle for any of you!"

Everyone laughed and we poured another round.

That night, Brownie brought in a basin of water and placed it down beside my bed. "Here, get washed."

"Oh?" I looked at him. "Why are you bringing me water? There must be a new star in the sky."

Brownie smiled. He lay down on his bed, threw me a cigarette, and lit one for himself. "Well, you're a teacher now."

"Teacher or not, I'm scared I've forgotten how to write. I hope I don't make a complete fool of myself."

"How could you forget? It's like swimming or riding a bike. Once you've learned you never forget."

Staring up at the thatched roof I whispered under my breath, "The character for earth under the character for black makes the character for ink. The character for *de* written *this* way joins a noun or an adjective to another noun. The character for *de* written *that* way joins an adjective to a verb. The character for *de* written the *other* way ... shit, how is that *de* used?"

"Stop worrying. At least you know there are such things as nouns and adjectives, which is good enough for teaching. I don't even know that much. I came here right from primary school, and even then all we read was Mao's *Quotations*. There's no hope for me, dammit!"

It was getting late and we went to bed. I stayed awake for a long time, wondering why they wanted me for a teacher, my nervousness growing. But I also felt quite self-important as, after all, someone thought highly of me, though I didn't know who.

The next morning there was a heavy mist and the valley was chilly and damp. While I was slipping on a new pair of nylon socks, the thick calluses on the soles of my feet caught at the nylon, making a strange squeaking sound. I changed into clean clothes, deliberately pulling the white collar a little higher, and put on a new pair of army shoes. I washed my face and hands, prepared to set out. As I was about to pick up my roll, Brownie snatched it, heaved it onto his back, and then bent over to pick up my bag that contained my washbasin and other things. I felt a bit awkward and grabbed my knife from him as we left together.

The others had collected in the yard, ready for the day's work up the mountain, looking like a bunch of monkeys in their ragged old clothes. Embarrassed, I tried to duck down and slip by, but they saw me.

"You idiot! What are you taking that knife for? Throw it away and try to look like a teacher!"

Gripping my knife even more tightly, I split open a stumpy little tree by the roadside with a single swipe.

Everyone cheered. "That's the spirit! Let them have it if they misbehave!"

I raised my knife in farewell and walked on with Brownie.

The school was some three miles from our village along the mountain path, and we reached it within an hour. As the school came into view, my heart started thumping and I hid my knife in my sleeve.

I stopped a local to ask directions to the administrative office. He lead us to a hut where we peered through an empty window frame. Someone inside noticed us and came out. "Are you here to register?" I nodded and he waved us in.

The man was very friendly and brought us a couple of chairs and some hot water. There were also two women in the room, presumably teachers, sitting at their desks correcting exercise books. They raised their heads to look at me, eyeing me from head to foot. Brownie and I sat down. We couldn't help inspecting the office the same way. It was just a thatched hut, not much different from the ones we had left except it had a few desks.

The man who had welcomed us smiled. "Everything okay?" He spoke with a heavy Cantonese accent. "You're quick! We only sent out the notification yesterday. We're slightly short-staffed at the moment. One of our teachers was transferred a few days ago and we need to fill his position. We did a search and discovered that you're the only one among the Educated Youths in the whole branch farm who has actually finished his secondary education. So we requested you."

Now I understood why I had been chosen. "I actually never finished, still had one year left," I said. "And as I've never taught before, I'm not sure if I'm any good at it. How should I address you?"

The man laughed. "My name's Chen Lin. Just call me Chen. As

for teaching, nobody is born knowing how to teach, you learn as you go along."

"I'm afraid I may not be worthy of the new generation."

"Don't talk like that. Here, have some water."

Forgetting that the knife was still in my sleeve, I reached out for the bowl of water. The knife slipped out and clashed to the floor. Some children at the window burst out laughing. It wasn't yet time for class and they had come to take a look at the new teacher. Blushing, I picked up the knife and leaned it against the desk. As I lifted my head, I saw a copy of the pocket-sized *New Chinese Dictionary* on Chen's desk.

"Good," said Chen, eyeing the knife. "We also do manual labor here at school—it's good you brought your knife along."

"You do manual labor here at school?" repeated Brownie.

"What do you think? Even here we have to re-thatch the roof and grow our own vegetables. We also take the children to work up in the mountains."

"Is that so?" I said. "Brownie, bring along my mattock next time you come."

Brownie stroked his face, not saying a word.

After we chatted for a bit, Chen looked out the window and stood up. "Well, let's get you settled."

Brownie and I stood up hastily and followed him out.

School was about to start and the children were making the most of their freedom, playing on the open dirt in front of the classrooms, running around and shrieking at the top of their voices. I hadn't been to school in nearly ten years, and scenes like this were a dim memory. I smiled and let out a nostalgic sigh.

Brownie stared in disbelief. "Hmmm … this isn't going to be easy for you."

Behind the classrooms there was a long row of thatched huts in front of which stood five wooden posts connected with a length of wire that was hung with bedding, assorted rags, and some brightly colored blouses. Chen motioned toward one door and pointed inside.

"Here's your room. There's a bed, a desk, and a bench. With a little cleaning you'll be comfortable enough."

I squeezed inside. At first it was too dark to see anything, then gradually I could make out a small, box-like area. The walls were made of split bamboo, covered with a layer of newspaper peeling at the edges. Against one wall was a low desk with a cavity for drawers but no drawers; however, the bottom of the cavity was still there for me to store my books and things. A few pictures were on the wall above the desk, and also a tattered calendar showing Li Tiemei—the lower half of her body missing—holding aloft a red lantern. The floor was littered with scrap paper and a short bench was on its back. A ramshackle wooden bed consisting of some wooden planks was pushed against the opposite wall.

I raised my head and gazed at the ceiling: a single thatched roof covered the whole building, which was partitioned into several small rooms by thin bamboo walls. The white top of the mosquito net next door was visible above the partition, and the roof-ceiling was crisscrossed with spider webs. It was as if I hadn't left production team quarters.

"That doesn't leak?" I asked Chen, staring at the thatch.

Chen was surveying the room with a smile on his face, turning over the paper on the floor with his foot. When he heard my question, he craned his neck and looked up.

"No, we re-thatched it only last year. If it does leak, you only have to reach up with a stick and spread the straw around a little bit. That should fix it."

Brownie dumped my things on the desk and gave the bed a kick.

"The cheap bastard," he said with vehemence, "he even took the bed mats with him. Chen, does the school have any? Could you give him a couple?"

Chen looked surprised. "You haven't brought your own? The school can't supply mats. The bed is school property, but people bring their own mats; and of course they take them when they move out. The desk and the chair are ours, too, so they can't be taken."

Brownie looked at me, rubbing his head.

"I guess I'll have to go back with you to get my bed mats," I said.

"Okay, then you can pick up your mattock, too," said Brownie. "I thought you were in for an easy life here."

I laughed. "It's still up in the mountains, how easy did you think it could be?"

"Since you've brought your knife," Chen said, "why don't you go cut some bamboo from the hills behind here, split it, and sleep on that?"

"Fresh bamboo is damp, it's no good for bedding. I'll just retrieve my mat."

The school bell outside started ringing.

"You two tidy up," said Chen. "I'm off to monitor." He squeezed through the door and walked away, swinging his arms.

Brownie and I swept the litter out of the room and lit the pile on fire. Then we trimmed the newspaper on the walls. The room now looked clean and attractive. I wanted Brownie to rest on the bench, but he refused and sat on the desk, leaving the bench for me.

Feeling quite cheerful I passed him a cigarette, helped myself to one, lit both, and took a long drag. Slowly I lowered myself onto the bench. The next moment I was sprawled on the floor. I sat up and looked: only three legs of the bench were in place— the fourth was lying on the floor.

Brownie shook with laughter. I saw the desk was also beginning to wobble so I scrambled to my feet and told Brownie to get off. We both sat on the bed planks.

II

That afternoon I started teaching. Chen called me to his office and handed me a worn textbook, a box of chalk, red ink, blue ink, a steel nib pen, and a notebook.

"Don't lose the textbook," he said. "It's nearly impossible to re-place."

The book was filthy, curled and folded so many times it was limp. Its thick clamminess in my hands disgusted me, and when I opened it up there were notes written in pen and pencil, and even chalk dust inside. "Whose book was this? He didn't have a disease, I hope."

The women teachers in the office laughed. "Of course he did."

I looked at them and saw that their books were perfectly clean. I held mine by the spine and shook it. Even Chen began to laugh. "What's this about disease? Li, the teacher who left, may have been a bit disorganized and unkempt, but he never lost the book. That says something. Look, here's the timetable."

He passed me a sheet of paper. One glimpse and my heart lurched. "What?! The final year of junior high? I only completed the first year of senior high! How can I teach the third year of sec-ondary school? The transitioning year!"

Chen smiled. "What do you mean? Just teach, that's all, it's not hard."

I firmly refused, giving lots of reasons, the most important be-ing that my educational background was inadequate.

Chen rubbed the desk with his finger. "Well, who's going to do it, then? Me? I've only finished primary, I'd be even worse. Why not give it a try? Try and we'll see."

I noted that this class was preparing for their final exams, and that it was extremely difficult to make it into the senior years.

"So what? There is no senior high here anyway. When they've finished this year, that's it. Come on, give it a try."

My heart was thumping but I said nothing.

Chen gave a sigh of relief and stood up. "Class starts soon, I'll take you to yours."

I still wanted to argue but I saw the other teachers in the office were looking at me curiously. "What's there to be afraid of?" one of them said. "We're not that brilliant either but we still teach, don't we?"

I wanted to say more but the bell rang. Chen stepped out, beckoning me. I had no choice but to pick up the teaching materials and hurry out after him. He stopped in front of one of the huts, saying, "Enter."

It looked dark inside, and I could only make out a few students sitting near the door gazing at me. I felt as if I were being led to the slaughter and was about to step through the doorway when, in a panic, I remembered something.

"What lesson are they up to?" I whispered to Chen.

Chen thought for a while. "Term's just started, they're probably still on the first lesson."

A low hum came from inside now, and Chen went in.

"Today you have a new teacher," he shouted. "Now be quiet, you hear me? You'll find yourself in trouble if you don't behave! Today you have a new teacher. See that you pay attention!"

His speech finished, he came back outside. I realized it was up to me now, so I gritted my teeth and stepped in. I was hardly inside the door when I heard a shout: "Stand up!" Desks and chairs clattered and the whole class was on their feet. I stopped dead. Another shout, followed by desk-and-chair clatter, and the class sat down again.

"The teacher didn't tell us to sit," someone yelled, "why did everyone sit down?" Once again the clatter followed.

"Sit down, sit down." I said quickly. The class broke out in laughter and sat down, causing more clatter.

I walked over to the desk in front of the blackboard, put down my things, slowly raised my head, and looked at my students.

It was a rare sight up in the mountains: so many kids with wild hair and dirty faces sitting together as if waiting to be fed. The desks and chairs were crude, unpainted, and yet too grimy to see the real color of the wood. The chairs were actually long benches made of logs split in half, rubbed smooth by pupil bottoms as if waxed. Dozens of eyes stared brightly at me. The kids sitting in the front row were really small, and seemed too young to be finishing their final year of junior high. The ones sitting in the back, however, were in need of a shave and possessed prominent Adam's apples.

Gathering up my courage I cleared my throat. "Ummm ... let's begin. What lesson are you on?"

As soon as the words left my mouth I felt embarrassed. This was not the sort of question a teacher should be asking. But the students didn't seem to notice, and a noisy babble broke out.

"Lesson one!"

"Lesson one!"

"We're up to lesson two!"

I picked up the heavy textbook and turned to lesson two. "Everyone turn to page four." But I didn't hear anyone open a book. I looked up at them still gazing at me. No one moved.

"Turn to page four," I repeated. Still no response from the class. I could feel the anger already rising inside me and pointed at the boy sitting nearest me. "Where's your book? Take it out and turn to page four."

He looked up. "What book? Teacher, we don't have any books."

The rest of the class joined in, shouting that they didn't have any books.

I looked around—sure enough, not a book in sight. I lost my temper and banged my book down on the desk. "No books? How do you expect to get any work done if you come to school without your books? Who's the prefect?"

A skinny little girl with brown streaks in her hair stood up. "Please sir, we don't have any books," she said timidly. "Each class Mr. Li copied the lesson on the blackboard. He copied out the day's lesson and then we copied it in our exercise books."

Shocked, I thought for a minute. "Doesn't the school issue you textbooks?"

"No, sir."

For a moment I lost it. "Hah! Officials without offices and schools without schoolbooks. Is going to school just a big joke then? When I went to school, the first thing you did at the start of the year was to collect your books, brand new ones, and make jackets for them. You took them to school every day—these books for this class, those books for that class. All right, I'll go talk to the principal. This is ridiculous!"

I left the hut to find Chen.

Chen was conscientiously marking homework. "Need something?" he asked when he saw me enter.

I drew a deep breath. "It's not me that needs anything. The school's forgotten to hand out textbooks to the students."

He laughed. "Ah, I forgot, I should've told you. There aren't any books. We're small fry up here. We order books but by the time we make it to town to collect them they're usually all gone. They say they can't print that many, so there is never enough to go around. We received a few books for the other grades, which the pupils share. But most still have to copy. It's not like in the big cities."

This seemed very odd to me. "Why can't the state print enough books for everyone? It's not like there's a shortage of paper! The production team receives piles of Criticism and Study materials. Why can't they print enough textbooks?"

Chen's face became stern. "Mind what you're saying. Mass criticism can't be relaxed, it's a 'matter of national interest.' If there's a shortage of textbooks, it must be that the country's in difficulties. A little copying here and there, and we can overcome. Correct?"

Realizing that I had said the wrong thing, I muttered a few words under my breath and returned to class. When I entered the room, the children fell silent, gazing at me.

I picked up the textbook. "Fine, let's copy."

They took out their exercise books, which were a variety of shapes and sizes, and opened them. Leaning forward or slouched back on their benches, they held their pens and waited.

I turned to lesson two, grabbed a piece of chalk, turned around, wrote the title on the blackboard, and proceeded to copy out the text sentence by sentence. Concentrating hard, the class copied the copy.

Someone far up in the mountains was bellowing at a cow, the sound drifting in faintly. My attention wandered as it occurred to me that the cow might have eaten something it shouldn't have and was being driven away. With the team I used to spend a lot of time herding cattle. Cows are extremely stubborn beasts but they're also very tolerant; they blink slowly and continue to graze where they like, no matter how hard you hit them or how loud you swear at them. Philosophers must be like this, too, or else how could they get ahead in their profession? But even these "philosophers" could sometimes be swayed, as when I'd go pee. Cows have a craving for salty things and as urine is salty, the cows would jostle each other to drink my urine. Then they became very happy. Sometimes I even held it in, saving my urine for the cows when we went up the mountain—not a drop would be wasted. After you feed cattle with your own urine you find that they obey you loyally, as if you were their father. I even used to feel like a party leader, happily using my pee as the source of my power.

"Sir, what does 'cow water' mean?" someone abruptly asked.

I came to my senses, rubbed off what I had written, and returned to copying the text.

The whole blackboard was covered and the students were still writing. I put down the textbook and watched them. Automatically clasping my hands behind my back, I began to feel quite cheerful: children were easier to look after than cattle.

When the children finished copying the passage, they would naturally expect some explanation from me, I thought to myself. As I cleared my throat, the students in the classroom next to us began to sing. The sound was ear-shattering. It was a song currently being paraded by the authorities, and it sounded exactly like people quarrelling. They sang so loudly that the roof thatch shook. Through the cracks in the bamboo partition I could see one of the women teachers urging them on. The children were probably bored stiff and sang as a way to let off steam, yelling at the top of their voices.

Not knowing what to do, I turned to look at the class. Nobody showed the least sign of alarm, though they began to whisper to each other and grow a little restless. When the singing next door stopped I tried to start talking again, but the recess bell rang. I shook my head. "Class dismissed."

"All rise!" the prefect shouted.

The children clattered up and rushed out the door.

As I followed them I saw the female teacher coming out too. "Was that your music class?" I asked.

She looked at me. "No, it wasn't."

"Then why was your class singing? They were so loud I couldn't teach."

"It was just before break time. A song now and then keeps the students' spirits high. They only sang for a couple of minutes. You can do the same with your class."

The yard in front of the classrooms looked the same as when I arrived—children of all ages rushing back and forth, kicking up dust. Soon the bell rang again. The children straggled back to the classroom and took their seats. The prefect shouted again to rise and the class stood up.

I sighed. "You don't even have books, what's the point of standing up so often? Forget it, just sit down and let's finish with what's on the board."

I walked up and down the room while the class continued copying. Because the benches were joined together it wasn't easy walking to the back rows, so I kept to the space in front of the blackboard. Not wanting to block the students' view, I moved over to the side and stood by the door. After a while I became bored.

Without the children, the yard looked deserted. Bright sunshine reflected off the dirt. A little piglet trotted by, came to a sudden halt, thought earnestly for a moment, then slowly ambled on still deep in thought. Absorbed in its progress, I began to count its steps. Suddenly the piglet broke into a trot again and my counting became muddled.

Feeling vexed, I noticed a hen pecking for food in the near distance. A cock was circling the hen but she paid no attention, pretending she didn't know he was present. The cock eventually drew near, quivered from head to foot, and turned bright red. The hen scurried away and resumed her aloof pecking. The cock shook his feathers and strutted forward with his head thrown back. Glancing from left to right in a dignified manner, he slowly advanced in a roundabout way. Gleefully I focused my full attention on the cock to see how he would fare.

"Teacher, I've finished copying," one of the children chimed.

I turned to see several pairs of eyes staring at me.

"Has everyone finished?" I asked.

"No! No!" some shouted.

Telling them to hurry up I resumed my watch, only to find that both the cock and the hen were shaking their feathers, their business completed. Feeling a pang of regret, I brought my attention back to the class, smiling at myself as I checked to see how many were still copying.

One by one the students raised their heads to look at me. Now it was my turn. At a loss for words, I finally said, "You've all finished copying, but do you understand what it says?"

They continued to stare at me. No one answered.

"The text is very simple," I tried again. "It's a story about a village. Can't you understand it?"

The students were silent.

Without meaning to I raised my voice. "What? That's odd. You've been learning to read for so many years, you should be able to read stories. You couldn't find a easier text than this." I pointed at one boy. "You. Say something."

The boy stood up hesitantly. He looked at me, then at the blackboard, then at the class, and grinned. "I can't," he said, and sat down.

"On your feet! How can you not understand? An easy story like this? You're not a fool."

The boy stood up again, looking a little uncomfortable, then said, "If I could read it, what's left for you to teach?"

The class laughed.

Irritated, I explained, "A landlord was carrying out sabotage and was exposed by the poor and lower-middle class peasants. Production in this village subsequently increased. Is it so hard to understand? What is there to teach? Unbelievable!"

I pointed to the prefect. "You try."

She stood up and slowly repeated from memory, "A landlord was carrying out sabotage and was exposed by the poor and lower-middle class peasants. Production in that... in this village went up."

"You learn fast, don't you?"

No sooner were the words out of my mouth than a student at the back said loudly, "What kind of teacher are you! I've never seen anyone teach the way you do. Why don't you teach the way you're supposed to! First you give us the new words, then divide the text into sections, then explain the main idea in each section, then the overall theme and the composition method. Show us which parts we have to learn by heart and which are for homework. Even I can teach like this! I bet you were a lousy worker in the team. You only came here to take it easy."

I looked at the boy, seeing only a big head, a contrastingly scrawny neck, and the whites of his eyes flashing as they rolled in the dim light. He spoke at an even pace, and when he was finished he wiped his mouth with his hand and grunted. The class was staring at me in silence.

I stood there stupidly, trying to think what to do. "Roll call! Everybody give me your names!"

Still no one spoke, so I pointed at the student sitting at the left end of the front row. "You. Name." The students reported their names in turn.

Then it was his turn, and I said, "Wang Fu, you said even you could teach. Well, come and show me."

Wang Fu stood up and fixed his eyes on me. "Is this a way of punishing me?"

"No, I'm not going to punish you. I'm new to the school, I was given the textbook right before class—this textbook. To be honest, I can read well enough but I've never taught before, and I don't know how to teach you. Now you tell me. How did Mr. Li teach you?"

Wang Fu relaxed. "How can I really teach?"

"Come here and stand in front of the blackboard. First, which words haven't you learned? I don't know how many words you've learned to write so far."

He thought about this for a moment, then made his way to the front.

Wang Fu was wearing a short jacket that left half of his arms bare. His creased pants were also short, and his bare feet were huge. When he picked up the chalk, I could see his hands were huge, too.

"Underline the words you don't know."

Wang Fu read through the text and slowly underlined a few words, then returned to his seat in the back row.

"All right, let me explain these words."

"There's some others I don't know!" yelled one of the students. Others started shouting the same.

"Okay, all of you! You can each come forward and underline the new words," I said.

The students scrambled forward to pick up the chalk. Jostling in front of the blackboard they underlined large chunks of the text. At a rough glance, it seemed that two-thirds of what was on the blackboard was unintelligible to them.

"How did you even make it to secondary school?' I laughed.

"No wonder you don't know what the lesson is about. Half these words you should have learned in primary."

Wang Fu's voice rose up from the back row. "We've never been taught the words I underlined. I can prove it."

"How about this,' I said, glancing over the blackboard, "I'll explain all the underlined words first, then we'll go through the new ones again more slowly."

The class agreed.

By the time I went through each word one by one, another class began to sing at the top of their voices. A day's work was almost over.

"Okay, let's sing a song, too. What songs do you know?"

The children yelled out their suggestions. I chose one, the prefect sang out the keynote, and dozens of throats produced an earthshaking noise. As I was gathering up my teaching materials, I thought these two periods had been quite fruitful; at the very least I had given them a solid grounding in a few words. It was like a workday up on the mountain—a few square feet cleared with your mattock and the record keeper arrives to calculate the area and meticulously note it down in his account book.

The bell rang as the singing ended. I looked at the prefect. "Class dismissed."

"What about homework," she asked. "You're supposed to give us some homework!"

I thought it over. "Your homework is to memorize today's new words. I'll test you tomorrow. Okay, that's it."

The prefect shouted "All rise." The children stood up with a clatter and rushed out ahead of me. As Wang Fu passed by, I asked him to stop. Looking a bit bewildered, he stared outside the door, walked over, and stood in front of me.

"You said you could prove which characters are really new ones," I said. "How can you do that?"

When he realized this was my question, he cheerfully said, "Each year, after I copy every text, I copy all the new words out again in another exercise book. This way I can keep count of how many words I know. Let me show you." He made his way carefully back to his desk and took out a cloth bundle, undid the four knots, took out an exercise book, retied the bundle again, and put it back in his desk. He returned to the front and handed the book to me. I opened it and saw that it was given as a prize for diligence in studying Mao's *Works*, and that the first page was inscribed with the name Wang Qitong.

"Ahhh," I said to myself. I knew this Wang Qitong.

Wang Qitong's nickname was Loose Shit. To call him Loose Shit was extremely odd because although Wang Qitong wasn't tall he was very solid. He could speed by you with a two-hundred pound sack of rice on his shoulders; there was no loose shit about him. I met him one day when we went to town to get our grain rations. The grain had to be brought by tractor from the granary in town, about forty miles away, to the mountains. The granary was enormous, the rice piled up like a mountain itself. Sacks were filled with bamboo pans, and then loaded onto the trailer.

That day two of our production teams had jointly sent out one tractor for grain. As we boarded the trailer in the morning our team quartermaster said with a grin to someone from team three, "Is Loose Shit here?" The man named Loose Shit sat huddled in a corner of the trailer, not saying anything. I happened to be sitting across from him and saw that his clothes were old and worn. The dirt around his ears had formed a thick crust, his face bore a fierce expression, and his hands and feet were remarkably large. I couldn't help feeling wary about him.

People from both teams were passing cigarettes around but no one offered him one. I thought for a moment and pointed at the cigarette in my hand, asking, "Want a smoke?"

He turned his eyes toward me and the fierce expression on his face instantly softened. He nodded, rubbed his hands vigorously on his pants, and reached for the cigarette.

The quartermaster from team three saw this. "Loose Shit, smoking won't bring back your tongue." Everyone laughed. I examined him, puzzled. He blushed, took out some matches, lit his cigarette, inhaled deeply, exhaled, and lowered his head. The slender white cigarette looked as if it had been inserted into the fork of a tree.

When we got stuck in the mud halfway there, of course it was Loose Shit who had to climb down, the rest of us sitting there as if unaware. With a great heave he single-handedly lifted the side of the tractor. The tractor rumbled a few times, eased forward, and continued to move. He ran after the trailer, hooked his arm over the tailboard, swung himself over, and sat down with a bump. The others were still laughing and talking as if nothing had happened. He could have been a tool for a machine, useful only when the machine broke down.

Since I didn't leave the mountains often and hadn't ridden the tractor more than a few times, I hopped off with him to push when we got stuck a second time. As the tractor moved forward, I chased after it with him. He swung himself up, but I was new to this maneuver and couldn't even grab hold of the tailboard. After Loose Shit sat down, he saw me still running behind and bent toward me, grunting weirdly. I shouted and the others realized what was happening. Finally, the driver stopped. Loose Shit remained bent toward me until I climbed in, then sat back down and smiled.

We arrived at the granary. The quartermaster jumped out to take care of formalities, while the rest of team three, save for Loose Shit, rushed into town to buy things. Our team entered the granary and fumbled about, filling our sacks. We were almost done when we noticed Loose Shit filling sacks on the other side of the granary all by himself. He was almost done, too, zipping along with the hundred-pound sacks on his back. Soon, the guys from team three returned with their purchases. They threw their last few bags into the trailer and we headed for the center of town.

This time our team hopped off to shop, while the other team

hurried off to buy more. Except, once again, for Loose Shit who was left behind to watch the tractor.

I jumped down and raised my head to ask, "Aren't you going to buy anything?"

He shook his head. He seemed to be content just sitting there on the sacks.

As I walked away, I asked the quartermaster, "What's the mute's name?"

"Wang Qitong."

"Why is he called Loose Shit?"

"Loose Shit is loose shit."

"But Loose Shit is much more useful than the hard shit in your team."

The quartermaster laughed. "That's why he's the only one I bring to help with the grain."

I thought this was strange. "The others didn't come to help?"

He looked at me. "They came on their own private business."

"That's a bit rough, bringing one man to fetch grain for the whole team so you only have to pay one man for the work."

He smiled. "It saves trouble."

I wandered around and bought an extra pack of cigarettes. When I returned I saw Wang Qitong still sitting in the trailer. I threw the pack toward him.

"Go get something to eat. I've already had something."

Wang Qitong caught the cigarettes with his free hand and pointed to his mouth, then to his stomach. He must have brought food with him, I thought. I climbed into the trailer and reclined on the sacks.

Feeling a nudge, I turned my head and saw Wang Qitong placing the pack of cigarettes beside me. The pack had been torn open and he was holding one cigarette between his fingers. I sat up.

"They're for you," I said, and threw the pack back to him.

He took it, bent over, and placed it beside me again. I took out a cigarette, lit it, and puffed slowly, looking at him.

When all the shoppers returned, the quartermaster said to Wang Qitong, "They still don't have the dictionary you want."

Wang Qitong grunted and a sad air filled his eyes. His hands, which reminded me of pineapples, slackened, and it seemed as if he was filled with the weariness of the day's hard work.

The driver started up and we took the road back to the mountains, first dropping our team off. After we had unloaded our grain, I came back outside just in time to wave goodbye to Wang Qitong as he disappeared into the distance.

Realizing that Wang Fu was Wang Qitong's son, I said, "I've met your father, he's a terrific worker."

Wang Fu blushed a little and remained silent. I leafed through the exercise book and saw page after page covered with densely written characters, listed one after another. I read through the list with great interest.

"Good. How many characters total?" I asked Wang Fu.

"Including the ones we learned today?"

I was taken aback for a moment and then nodded.

"Including the ones today, there's altogether three thousand four hundred and fifty-one."

I was amazed. "That precise?"

"You can count if you don't believe me."

I opened the exercise book again.

"One, two, three, four, five, six, seven, eight, nine, ten. Do you count these ten numbers as ten characters?"

"Of course. What are they if they're not ten characters? Are they one character?"

I laughed. "Then three thousand four hundred and fifty-one would count as three thousand four hundred and fifty-one characters."

Wang Fu didn't get my joke. He said earnestly, "After ten comes a hundred, a thousand, a million, a billion. We haven't learned the character for billion yet, but I know it. I've written all the characters I've learned myself which aren't in the textbook into another exercise book. There's four hundred and thirty-seven."

"You take your studies very seriously," I said. "I have no idea how many characters I've learned."

"You're our teacher, of course you know more."

The bell rang again. I gave the exercise book back to Wang Fu and returned to the main office.

When Chen saw me come in he asked with a smile, "How was it? Not too bad? It's bound to be a bit rough at the beginning. You'll get used to it soon."

I sat down at the desk assigned to me and put the textbook down. After a little thought I asked Chen, "Are there any rules for teaching this class? I can see you can't really make it up as you go along. Since the National Textbook Unification reform, textbooks for each subject have been the same throughout the whole country, but there should also be a unified standard for teaching or people won't know if they're teaching properly. For example, how many sections should a text be divided into? What is the main idea of each section? What is the overall theme? What is the composition method? I might interpret these things one way, but another school might teach it another way. Language isn't like math—one plus one makes two wherever you are in the world. Language courses should have rules so that we can be on firm ground."

"Yes, you're right," Chen said. "They do have what they call teachers' manuals, written by high officials, some even edited at the provincial level. But it's even harder for us to buy those books."

I laughed. "Tell me who has one and I'll go and copy it."

Chen looked outside. "It's difficult."

"Well, I guess I'll just have to play it by ear. And I won't bother about any rules."

Chen sighed. "Do what you can. According to the regulations, no one can have a salaried job until they're eighteen. So even if these children weren't in school there's no work for them anyway.

They are certainly better off learning something here."

With that off my mind, I bent over my desk and started reading through the textbook lesson by lesson.

The class became easier to teach within the week, though inevitably I often wondered about what I was doing. I decided that learning to write was the main task, and using Wang Fu's exercise book as a model I proceeded character by character, naturally including composition. Initially, the students' compositions looked like hieroglyphics; I would often be up until midnight trying to decipher their handwriting. Their compositions also were usually less than a paragraph, most written in some form of current jargon that put you to sleep. Then I reminded myself that I wasn't reading a novel and felt a bit more at ease while at the same time growing more and more doubtful that the children would find any use in being able to write like this.

The school day was hectic but my life was desolate at night. After only a week, I began to miss my friends and decided to visit the team on Sunday.

Brownie was very happy to see me. He patted his bed, told me to sit down, and went off to find the others. Of course we discussed what we should eat, some disappearing straightaway to find provisions. When Laidi heard the news she joined the rest of us inside. She examined me up and down, then sat next to me on the other side of the bed. The bed sagged, and Brownie jumped up, saying "My bed can't take three people!"

Laidi, however, settled her whole weight on the bed. "Then buzz off so that I can have a nice cozy chat with our teacher."

Everybody laughed; Brownie squatted on the floor.

Toying with her hair, Laidi said tenderly, "See how pale you've gotten teaching indoors."

I brushed away Laidi's dumpy outstretched hand. "Keep your hands to yourself."

"Well! We've really floated up in the world, haven't we?" Laidi exclaimed. "We laboring people can't come near you now. Let me tell you: you can teach for a hundred years, I still know what you've got between your legs! Huh! Just a few days and he fancies himself a scholar!"

I smiled. "A scholar? Me? My students are more learned than me. You know Wang Qitong, team three's Loose Shit? He has a son, Wang Fu, who's in my class. Wang Fu knows three thousand eight hundred and eighty-eight characters. I made a fool of myself the first day—it was him who taught me how to teach."

No one believed me, so I described what had happened.

"So it's true," they said. "How many characters do we know? Anyone counted?"

"I have an idea," I said. "When I was at school, my Chinese teacher saw that some of us were getting bored with studying, so he said, 'I don't know what talents you might possess in other fields, but we focus on literacy. Here's a *New Chinese Dictionary*. Open it to any page you like. If you can't find a single word that you're unable to read, write, and explain the meaning of, then I'll give up, you can play in class as much as you like and if I interfere you can call me an old bastard.' None of us believed him, so we eagerly picked up the dictionary and opened it. But he was right. There were characters that looked familiar but we couldn't pronounce, or characters we thought we knew how to pronounce but on checking, we discovered we were wrong; and there were even more characters we didn't know or couldn't explain. We gave up. Later, we found out that the teacher used this method every year to straighten out his students—it worked every time."

The others didn't believe this either and started hunting around for a *New Chinese Dictionary* to try it out. But nobody seemed to have one. I said I didn't even have one at the school.

Laidi, who had kept silent, now drawled, "How can you call yourself the king of children without a dictionary! No worries, your old ma here has one."

"Then let's have it," I said hastily.

Laidi's face brightened. She lay back on the bed, propped herself up on her elbows, and crossed her fat legs. "Well, there are conditions."

Grinning, we asked her what conditions.

Laidi slowly rolled herself around and sat up. She reached for her shoes with her feet, stood up, straightened her clothes, tidied her hair, and sashayed toward the door, swinging her hips.

"Well, we don't want to be a Party Secretary, and we don't want to be a Party Committee Secretary, we only want to be a music teacher. How about it? Isn't a dictionary a fair exchange for a teacher, considering that your actual teacher doesn't have a dictionary!"

Everybody turned to me, laughing. I scratched my head.

"What's so precious about a dictionary? I can just buy one. Anyway, doesn't the principal, Chen, have one? I can borrow his."

Laidi stopped in the doorway. She turned back, looking a bit deflated, and thought for a moment.

"Seriously, Beanpole, what's the school's music class like? What songs are they teaching?"

I laughed and told them how the students' singing made me jump.

Hands on her hips, Laidi tossed her head. "They call that singing? That's ridiculous. I can tell you, those songs are for yelling, not for singing. Talk to the school when you get back, Beanpole, say there's a Laidi in our team who knows so many songs her head is about to explode. They can invite her to teach a few of her tunes, why not."

"I'm not part of the leadership, how can I grant approval?"

Laidi mulled this over. "Let's do it this way. You write the words and I'll write the music. Then you teach my song to your class. It's bound to be different from the songs the other classes sing. When the leaders asks about my song, just tell them Laidi composed it. Once they see how talented I am I bet they'll want me to teach the music course."

The others scoffed at Laidi's fantasy. Brownie stood up. "You think composing music's a game? You need a university degree, there's a special course. It's called art, get it? Art! You're completely nuts!"

Laidi blushed scarlet and looked at me.

"Well, I've only had a few years of schooling and now I'm teaching the third year of secondary," I said. "It's hard to predict how things might turn out, you can never be sure who can do what."

"What's so hard about composing?" Laidi snorted. "I'm always humming tunes to myself, and if I write them down that's music. To me it seems they sound better than the songs we have now."

Swaying her bottom over again, she plonked herself down on the bed and patted my shoulder. "How about it, Beanpole? That's what we'll do."

The people who had been scavenging for food returned. They brought dried bamboo shoots, eggplant, pumpkin, as well as some dried boar meat, not to mention a few bottles of liquor. Brownie split some firewood and Laidi put the pot on the stove. With a great banging and bustling, within half an hour ten dishes were prepared. We sat in a circle, eating and drinking leisurely as we gossiped about different rumors and local events that had us laughing and swearing.

"It's more fun here with the team," I said. "It's deserted at school after the children have gone home; it's very easy to feel lonely."

"I thought there were women teachers at the school," Laidi said.

"We do have a few highbrows, I don't know where they're from. At night they never make a sound."

Everyone sniggered. "What kind of sounds would you expect?" someone cracked.

I laughed too. "Anyway, they really are highbrows, they teach in a very proper and orderly sort of way. But me, how am I supposed to teach?"

"I agree with what you said: the basis of learning is reading and writing," Brownie said, sipping the liquor. "If you can read and write you can do anything."

"Students in the last year of junior high know more characters than us," someone said. "But I can't see that we've needed them, and these kids probably won't need them either."

"Around here," said Laidi, "you only need to learn enough to write letters and read newspapers, which is enough to write criticisms. Why go on year after year learning more simply because it's 'proper procedure'?"

"What if you can read and write but nobody understands you and you don't understand anyone else?" Brownie said. "The other day on the radio someone was explaining what illiteracy meant. Let me tell you, even if you can read and write you can still be illiterate if you don't understand what's being written. You're only literate when you can understand the different shades of meaning."

The others were unconvinced. "That can't be right!" someone said doubtfully. "The Campaign for Eradicating Illiteracy only involved learning how to read and write. Once you can read and write you're no longer illiterate. Aren't all of us Educated Youths?"

I thought it over. "If you can't read and write, that can be called *reading* illiteracy, but if you can't understand what you read that's *cultural* illiteracy. What Brownie heard is true, but it seems most people don't bother about the distinction."

"Of course, it was the BBC Chinese Service," Brownie said. "They explained it all very clearly."

Everyone laughed. Laidi stabbed a finger at Brownie's eyes.

"Brownie!" she shouted. "You've been listening to enemy radio! I'm going to tell the leadership!"

"Go ahead and tell them!" Brownie shouted. "Doesn't the Party Secretary listen, too? They report immediately whatever happens in China long before the rest of us get to know. When Baldy Lin died in Inner Mongolia our Party Secretary heard the news the very same day on his earphones. He kept it to himself for weeks, not sure if he should believe it or not. Then when the Center made the announcement he became very smug and said that *he* had known all along. In fact, everybody already knew but didn't dare talk about it. So where do all of *your* trashy songs come from, Laidi? Don't you learn them from enemy radio every day? The Beatles, ABBA, John Lennon—a load of old trash, that's what you've collected!"

Laidi pushed some food into her mouth. "Central Radio might not be that clear," she said, chewing away. "But who asked us if we wanted to be in the middle of nowhere! There may be a lot of interference on Central Radio, Brownie, but *I* still listen to it every day."

"If Central Radio gives you the first sentence I can recite you the second," Brownie said. "It's always the same old stuff, I know it forward and backward, I don't *need* to listen to it."

I laughed. "I guess the whole country's the same. All those editorial clichés, my class knows them inside and out, you don't need to teach them composition. If you ask them to write an essay on National Day, they copy last year's October first editorial word for word and it isn't in the least out of date."

The others nodded and said it was true. Brownie added that he could probably be a teacher, too.

"Of course," I said.

After the meal we were all a bit sweaty. Laidi piled the bowls and chopsticks into a washbasin and took them out to wash, while a few others swept the table scraps outside for the hens, pigs, and dogs to fight over. We all stood outside and gazed around at the mountains, our tongues poking around our mouths for the last bits of food. I watched the animals inhaling the scraps. They still looked the same as before, and I smiled involuntarily.

"A week in the mountains is a year at school. I feel as if I've been away for ages."

The Party Secretary was walking by some ways off and saw me. He put his hands behind his hips and smiled.

"You're back? How's the teaching going?"

"It's great."

He came over to us and accepted a cigarette from Brownie, lit it, and squatted down, puffing the smoke at a dog. The dog sneezed and left, wagging its tail.

"There's an old saying," he said. "'If you have rice in the bin for the following day, to be king of children is not worth the pay.' Do your students cause trouble?"

"There's not much leeway for that."

"I heard you're teaching the final year of junior high. That's great! In the old days if you finished primary you'd be a licentiate, and after junior high you'd be a recommended scholar. Finishing senior high would probably make you a principal scholar. To be a recommended scholar was pretty rare in those days— even if you didn't have an official position you'd still be a local big shot, everybody would be licking your boots. Now you're teaching future recommended scholars. That's impressive!"

I laughed. "One day your son will become a recommended scholar."

His face glowed. "Ah," he sighed, "how could he measure up to that standard! In the old days, recommended scholars had to pass exams, but the students now, they don't take exams, they just do what they like and then when they are old enough they come back to the team to work, barely knowing how to read and write. My son wrote a letter home and we received a letter back three days later. I asked him to read it to me, but he just mumbled something neither of us could understand."

Laidi returned with the clean bowls and chopsticks. When she heard this, she said, "So you're still going on about that letter. Shame on you!"

The Party Secretary smiled, saying nothing, and took a drag of his cigarette.

"He asked me to read what was written in the letter," Laidi told us. "I read it over and over again but it just didn't make sense. So I asked him, 'Whose grandfather are you?' and he said 'I'm not anyone's grandfather yet.' 'But this is addressed to someone's grandfather.' It turned out it was actually the letter his son had written, returned to the sender, and his son was pretending it was the reply he was reading. The address of the recipient was written in the middle of the envelope and the sender's address was on the side. The handwriting looked like dog prints, you couldn't make heads or tails of it, I bit my tongue trying to read it."

Everyone roared with laughter and even the Party Secretary joined in. "Oh well," he said cheerfully, "it's best not to talk about it."

I spent the rest of the day wandering around the farm, and after dinner prepared to head back to the school.

"Stay overnight," Brownie said. "You can set off tomorrow morning."

"No, I'd best go back now. I have to prepare for class which begins first thing tomorrow morning. I better give myself enough time."

Brownie said that sounded reasonable but he would walk with me anyway. I stopped him, however, saying that I'd be visiting often and I could walk back by myself. So Brownie saw me off as far as the edge of the village, where he waved goodbye and turned back.

Night was drawing close but there was still a streak of red clouds in the sky above the mountaintops. The dirt road through the forest was indistinct and I remembered the last few nights were moonless. I had three miles to go and I was afraid I'd be floundering in the dark, so I quickened my steps. A short distance later a figure abruptly appeared at the side of the road.

"Who's that?" I asked in alarm.

There was a laugh. "Anyone would think you're running to your own execution." It was only Laidi. I relaxed and walked on slowly.

"It's very late, what are you doing up here?" I asked.

"What do you mean? Hold on a minute. I want to ask you why you didn't say goodbye to your old ma when you left."

I smiled. "We've known each other for ages, there's no need to say goodbye. I'll be back often."

After a short silence, Laidi suddenly remarked in an odd voice, "Beanpole, is it true what you said?"

I was mystified. "What did I say?"

"We call you a highbrow and now you really pretend to be above everyone else! How can you have forgotten in less than one day?"

I gazed up at the sky, my eyes shifting back and forth, but still I couldn't remember. Laidi suddenly became shy and hummed a little tune. I had never seen her so coy. My heart pounded, my face grew hot, and my neck stiffened. I forced my head down.

Laidi sighed. "You mean you've really forgotten? Didn't you talk about writing a song?"

I felt the blood freeze in my veins, and I cursed myself silently.

"What do you mean I've forgotten. It was you who talked about it."

"Never mind who talked about it. What do you think?"

I had not taken the matter seriously. Now with Laidi being so earnest, I thought it over.

"Why not? It's just writing a song, isn't it? You write it and I'll teach my class to sing it." I suddenly felt inspired and licked my lips. "Sure. Let's write a song, something that will sound different. Great!"

Laidi was also excited. "Come on, your old ma will walk with you part of the way and we can think of some ideas."

"Don't keep calling yourself my old ma in front of your old pa. I'm older than you are."

Laidi laughed. "Fine. My old pa will write the words and your old ma will set them to music."

"I'm not sure if I can write the words."

"We've already settled it, you can't worm out of it now. No, you have to write the lyrics, that was the deal."

After a little thought, I said, "Anyway, I can't write anything now."

"Who said anything about now? The reason I snuck up on you out here is because Brownie and the others think that all I'm good for is making a fire and boiling rice, so I want to do something secretly, see, to make them back off."

The King of Children

I looked at the sky, which was almost completely dark. "All right, it's a deal. You wait for my lyrics. I have to go now." I walked on quickly.

I hadn't gone very far before I heard Laidi shouting after me.

"Beanpole! Look how stupid I am. I forgot the main thing."

I stopped and turned to look back. Laidi's shadow hurried closer and I felt a hard object poke against my belly. I grabbed it with both hands. It was square and warm from Laidi's hands.

"Here. This is the dictionary. It's for you."

I was at a loss and about to refuse, but then said gratefully, "Thanks, but don't you need it?"

"You use it," Laidi said in the dusk.

I couldn't think of what else to say, so I just said, "I have to go. Please go back."

I turned and walked off. After a while, I stopped to listen and then turned around and shouted, "Laidi! Please go back!"

There was a short silence in the darkness, followed by the sound of slow footsteps.

III

That night I spent a long time thinking about the song, but only hackneyed expressions kept popping into my mind. It was clear that I couldn't break free from clichés and I decided to go to bed. Then I thought of Laidi. She was certainly fat. I measured my own arms and legs, feeling ashamed, then began to count up to a hundred and eventually fell asleep.

When I woke the next morning I walked outside into the mist to fill my water bucket and wash up. After this, I felt quite energetic but didn't know what to do with myself, so I sat on the bed to smoke. I caught sight of the dictionary Laidi had given me, picked it up, and started to flip through it. Gradually, I began to find it more absorbing than a novel. It was only when the bell rang for class that I came back to earth and hurried off to the classroom.

The children had just sat down. After the ritual courtesies, I stepped in front of the blackboard.

"Pay attention now. I want to clarify exactly what you've been doing in school. This will be your ninth year studying Chinese ..."

"What do you mean, ninth year!" they shouted. "It's only been eight years!"

I questioned this and they told me they had attended five years of primary school. I had no idea that the educational reform had lopped off one year of primary education.

"Okay, eighth year. But your present level of Chinese is about the same as the last year of primary, maybe not even that. If you stay on this track, even another eight years won't bring much improvement. It might be better instead if you could make a real effort to start all over again. Take vocabulary, for example. Wang Fu has the statistics. You've learned more than three thousand characters. These three thousand characters ordinarily should be enough. But your compositions—I'm not talking about mistakes in writing characters—they're unreadable. If you're going to write something for other people to read, you have to make it legible and comprehensible, otherwise you might as well be sitting there farting."

The students tittered, but I continued solemnly.

"What's so funny about that? You're only hurting yourselves. In fact, it wouldn't hurt you to be a bit more serious. What I want now, with your writing, is that first, it has to be legible, never mind if it doesn't look good. Secondly—hmm, well, there is no secondly, only the first thing. Your writing must be readable. Everyone clear about this?"

"Yessir!" the class shouted at the top of their voices.

I smiled. "Determination isn't a matter of how loud you can shout. Under our rules, from now on, any character that's not written clearly will count as an error, and you'll have to copy it out fifty times."

The class groaned.

"Yes, I know. But think about it; it's for your own good. You'll have studied for eight years, won't you feel ashamed of yourselves if you leave school without being able write properly? You haven't had to take exams the last few years, you've just been wasting time. I'm not talking about the Great Truths, you know about those. I'm only trying to say that at the very least you should have some self-respect. Seeing that you've completed so many years of school, you should master a thing or two, it's your working capital.

"The second thing is that there's to be no more copying editorials when you write your compositions. No more copying, no matter what. So what do you write? Each time I will give you a topic ... no, wait, I won't give you an exact topic. What shall we do? You'll write on your own, write about some event, write about anything you like. You don't have to write much, but you must write honestly and clearly. Don't give me any of this flowery stuff, none of this 'Red flags flutter in the breeze, war drums shake the sky.' How many red flags have you seen? Who's ever heard a war drum? How could the broken old drum at the branch farm ever shake the sky? Cut out all this stuff, it's no use! Write about one event, clearly. For example, when you write about going to school, you describe how you get up in the morning, what you do next, how you go to school, what you see on the way...."

"The teacher before said that this was just record keeping!" one student shouted.

"What's wrong with record keeping? You're doing well if you can keep clear records. Forget you've been at school for nine years, just try it. Okay, let's start right now. Everybody, take out your pen and paper and we'll do some record keeping. Write ... write about going to school."

The class chattered noisily as they began to dig into their bags. Having talked so much at once, I felt a bit dizzy, but I was also much more cheerful, as if I had finally gotten something off my chest.

The class took out their pens and paper and began to write.

"Teacher, what do I write?" someone cried out.

A H   C H E N G

"Just write like I told you."

"I can't."

"Take it slowly, don't rush."

"I can't remember how I come to school."

Leaning against the door, I let my glance wander over the class—some of the children leaned forward, others slouched back.

"You'll think of something. No one knows more about what you've done than yourself."

The classroom became very quiet. The voice of the teacher next door pierced the air, very intense and precise. The simpler a thing seemed to be, the harder it was to do. I began to walk around slowly, watching the children as they wrote.

Suddenly Wang Fu raised his head. I looked at him, and in embarrassment he lowered it again and put down his pen.

"Have you finished, Wang Fu?"

He nodded.

I walked to the back row and picked up Wang Fu's paper. I saw the others had lifted their heads and were looking at Wang Fu.

"Has everyone finished?"

They hastily looked down and wrote on. I began to read Wang Fu's paper to myself. Each word was clearly and carefully written: *We don't have a clock at home, I got up, I got dressed, I washed my face, I had breakfast, I washed up, I took my school bag, I don't have a clock, I walked for a long time, there was mist in the mountains, I got to school, I sat down, class began.*

I couldn't help smiling. "Good," I said to him.

I went back to the front of the room and put the paper on my desk. The children raised their heads and looked at me.

"Who else has finished?"

Another boy handed in his paper and I read what he had written: *Go to school, walk, to the school classroom. I walk to school.*

"Good," I said again.

The children grew excited. Exchanging looks, they resumed writing.

More and more students handed in their papers. They began to talk, the noise level growing. At last the bell rang. I said class was dismissed but instead of leaving they rushed forward to ask me questions.

"Go outside and play. We can talk about it next period."

They still wouldn't disperse but discussed their papers among themselves. Wang Fu sat quietly in his seat, throwing me a questioning look every now and then.

The bell rang again and the children returned to their desks. I picked up Wang Fu's composition.

"Wang Fu wrote very well. First, there are no wrong words and it's legible. Second, it's got clear content. I'm going to read it aloud to you."

When I finished, the class started laughing.

"Don't laugh. It's true there are too many 'I's. One 'I' is quite enough for people to understand, there's no need to have more than one. He wrote about several actual events, and what's more he noticed the mist. No one else wrote about the mist. Overall it's clear, though there are too many commas, commas all through it. However, this is something easily corrected in the future."

I picked up the second paper and read it aloud. The class laughed again.

"It's funny, isn't it? Eight years in school and when he writes about something his writing is as twitchy as a rabbit's tail. But at least in this composition he wrote the word 'walk.' I know that he didn't run, nor did he fly, and he didn't get someone to carry him, but he walked. In this way, he'll gradually be able to write a little more and be a little clearer. It's much better than copying."

Wang Fu was very happy. His eyes flashed and he wiped his mouth. I read out the papers one by one, and everyone laughed from start to finish. Class ended and the children rushed out. I walked out slowly. The teacher next door appeared, too. She asked me, "What in the world were you reading? They laughed straight through the whole period."

"Let them laugh, it will save them making mistakes later on."

IV

I stopped teaching the textbook. Each day I simply gave them a few new words and suggested different things to write about. After a couple weeks, the children started complaining and getting restless. I couldn't help feeling hesitant, but seeing with my own eyes their writing improve—and though their work was awkward it was at least their own—I decided to keep tormenting them.

Another two weeks flashed by. The school deliberated on a major manual labor activity, the plan being to hew bamboo and wood to replace the rotten rafters in the huts. Since my class was the most senior, it was assigned the task of climbing up the mountain to collect the bamboo. When I told this to the class, there was an uproar as everyone wanted to go with their own team. I couldn't make up my mind. I asked Chen, who said we still had a few days before we started and we could decide then.

The day before the manual labor, I addressed the class at the end of the period.

"Tomorrow, everyone bring your knife. Our class is responsible for two hundred and thirty bamboo canes. Let's divide into groups today and each group elect a leader. We'll try to finish cutting down the bamboo in the morning so that we can carry it all back in the afternoon."

"Which team will we work with?" they asked.

"We'll work with mine. I'm familiar with them so we won't have to waste time organizing people together; we can start as soon as we arrive. But it's rather far and the boys will have to help the girls."

"Who needs them!" the girls cried. "It's a job we do all the time, we're just as good as them."

"Will we be assigned a composition about it when we get back?"

one student asked.

I smiled. "Don't think about that now, just do the job at hand. If you fill your mind with a lot of nonsense, you might have an accident."

"I bet we'll have to write about it. Mr. Li always used to give us this topic. He would always ask us to write a composition about every school activity. Why not tell us the topic now so that we can write it today?"

"Look, the activity hasn't even started yet. If you write about it you would certainly be copying."

Wang Fu looked at me, a faint smile on his face. "Set the topic and I can write the composition today, and it definitely won't be copying. Do you believe me?"

"Wang Fu, if you can write about how everyone drank to your parents at their wedding, then you can write today about how we're cutting bamboo tomorrow."

Everyone laughed, looking at Wang Fu.

Wang Fu raised his big hand. "Okay, I'll make you a bet."

"What will you bet?"

Wang Fu fixed his eyes on me. "You mean you'll really accept the bet?" he asked, blushing crimson.

Seeing the odd look on Wang Fu's face, I felt a moment's anxiety, but then thought there could hardly be any risk involved.

"Of course. And the whole class can stand witness."

The children were watching Wang Fu and me with rising excitement.

"Wang Fu," I said, "what's your bet?"

Wang Fu's eyes shone. He was about to speak but then dropped his head.

"I'll accept your bet," I said. "If I lose, you can have anything of mine you like."

The children began to shout at the same time. Some said he should take my pen; others, my dictionary. When Wang Fu heard the word dictionary, he cried out, "Teacher, I want the dictionary!"

My dictionary had already become a sacred object to the class. The children from better-off families had made a trip from the mountains to the local township to buy one, but there were none there, and the dictionary became even more sacred. At the beginning of each lesson I would put it on my desk as the authority. Wang Fu often borrowed it to look through. Sometimes he'd ask me about a random word and of course I couldn't always answer. Then he'd sigh and remark, "This is the teacher's teacher."

Knowing how much Wang Fu wanted the dictionary didn't bother me at all.

"By all means," I said, and passed the dictionary over to the class prefect.

The children looked from her to me in delight.

"Put it away safely," I said. "Don't let it get dirty."

Wang Fu rubbed his chest with both hands. "But there's one condition," he said slowly.

"Whatever you say."

Wang Fu fixed his glance on me again. "We have to do the job with my team, team three."

"No problem. Any team's fine, including team three. Don't imagine that because we're going to your team tomorrow you can write about the event today. Everybody will be witness to tomorrow's manual labor, and if it doesn't match with what you've written, you lose. You don't even know what the weather will be like tomorrow."

Wang Fu was not discouraged. "Fine. I'll wait for all of you at my team tomorrow."

Later that afternoon I whetted my knife. It was still light out and I sat in front of my door watching the teacher next door wash her hair.

I pondered a moment and remarked, "We're scheduled for manual labor tomorrow. What's the point of washing your hair today? It's a waste of effort."

"If it gets dirty I can wash it again, can't I? Tell me, which team are you going to join tomorrow?"

"Team three."

"Do they have more bamboo near team three?"

"Not necessarily. But I've made a bet with a student."

"Always something improper: betting with your students? Listen, the way you conduct your class every day is quite irresponsible, and I've heard that they've found out about it up at the Education Office; they say they're going to come and straighten things out! Seriously, you'd better watch your step."

I laughed. "How can they say I'm being irresponsible? I'm teaching them to write, character by character, there's not a grain of irresponsibility in that. If you're going to teach you might as well teach something useful."

She poured out the water, startling a hen nearby. Lifting up the wet hair hanging over her forehead while looking at me from the corner of her eye, she said, "You're not using the unified teaching materials. How do you think you're going to justify yourself when the inspector comes around?"

"That teaching material is unified all right, I can't even tell the difference between the Chinese lessons and the political lessons. My class is learning Chinese—what are they going to do when they return to their teams? Become party secretaries?"

"Well, it's character building, isn't it?"

"That's exactly it: I'm building up their characters."

She giggled. "Anyway, just watch your step!"

That evening I was totally bored with nothing to do. Then I remembered I had agreed to write a song with Laidi, so I took out a sheet of paper and began to scribble a few lines. I was in the middle of changing some words around when I suddenly couldn't remember how to write the character for "unworthy." I knew it perfectly well, but for some reason I just couldn't remember how to write it. I decided to ask Chen if I could borrow his dictionary.

I felt my way in the dark to his door. "Are you there, Chen?"

"Yes, I'm here," he called from inside. "Come in, come in."

I pushed open the door and entered. He was sitting at a low desk marking exercise books. When he saw it was me he said, "Take a seat. How's everything? All right?"

"I don't want to disturb you, I just wanted to check a character. Can I borrow your dictionary? I can use it here."

"Didn't you just get a dictionary?"

"Yes, but I made a bet with Wang Fu today. I bet my dictionary and left it with the stakeholder."

Chen smiled. "You still haven't rid yourself of old habits from team life. What are you doing betting with your pupils? Although we don't talk about the "dignity of the teaching profession" any more, we still have to exert our authority. If you lose the bet, I'm afraid you'll lose control over them."

"There's no way I can lose."

"How's that?"

"Wang Fu said that he could write about tomorrow's manual labor today. You think he can win? I've been trying to change the students' bad habits and help them write honestly, but he's hopeless. He's an extremely hard-working boy, but no matter how hard he works, he can't know what's going to happen tomorrow. You wait and see—I'll win."

Chen sat silently, tapping his desk.

"Whatever happens, you should be careful," he said, not looking at me. "There's no problem with the school; after all, you're still teaching, aren't you? But the Education Office has somehow found out that you aren't following the textbook. Actually, I think it's good to have a grasp of the fundamentals, but you shouldn't get too far off track, right?"

"The children will have little chance of an education beyond this class, to say nothing of the impossibility of university. When they return to their teams, they won't have wasted their school years if they can describe clearly whatever it is that they do. Isn't it obvious that it's only worthwhile studying something useful like this? Otherwise, it's really as people say: the more you do, the less use it is."

Chen sighed but said nothing.

I checked the word in the dictionary. Smiling at my poor memory, I said goodnight to Chen. The moon had risen late, and half of its yellow disc was hidden by mountain peaks, clear but not bright. I gazed up, suddenly overwhelmed with doubt. Wang Fu was an extremely serious student, why had he stood so firm today? A sense of foreboding filled me, as if something ominous was in the air itself. I thought it over again: how could anything happen? When I got back to my room I lay down on my bed. In the end I still felt that there was no way I could lose. On the contrary, I thought winning would be too easy.

The next morning I ate breakfast, grabbed my knife, gathered together the children from the various teams, and headed for team three. The dew was heavy along the mountain path. The children's bare, wet feet plopped along like a parade of people clapping their hands. Everyone was in high spirits, saying that Wang Fu was really an idiot, and they all wanted to be witnesses and not let him cheat me out of my dictionary.

We arrived at team three after walking nearly an hour. The team must have left for work because we couldn't see anyone, the place was deserted. In the distance, I saw a boy in shirt and pants too small for him standing at the end of the valley. I knew it must be Wang Fu. He slowly bent over to pick up a long piece of bamboo, balanced it on his shoulder, and walked toward us, swaying from side to side under its weight. When I could see that it was indeed Wang Fu, I was about to call him but then I watched him tilt his shoulder and drop the bamboo to the ground. Several stalks, each the diameter of a teacup, were piled in the grass beside the path. We walked closer.

"Are you carrying bamboo for your family, Wang Fu?"

Wang Fu looked at me with a grin. "I've won."

"We haven't started yet, how can you say you've won?"

Wang Fu wiped the moisture off his face. His hair stuck damply to his skull, and there was not a single dry patch to be seen on his sweat-darkened clothes, which clung to his body.

"Let's go," Wang Fu said. "I'll take you down the ravine, you can all be my witnesses."

The students looked at each other inquisitively. I tensed up. Looking around, I pressed ahead hesitantly with the class.

Humid air suffused the mountains, gradually ascending as mist. The sun moved through the mist in the shape of a white disc. In the forest the dew gathered on the leaves and fell drop by drop. As the mist grew denser, it fell like rain.

The view opened and we saw hundreds of long bamboo stalks scattered across the mountainside. A man was clearing off the side-shoots with a knife, his arm rising and falling. The noise echoed through the length of the ravine. We walked closer and slowly came to a halt. The man stopped cutting and turned around. A scowling face inspected us.

I recognized him at once: it was Wang Qitong. A slow smile appeared as he wiped his face; his features softened.

"What the hell are you are doing here, Wang?"

Wang Qitong gave a weird chuckle. He nodded to me and pointed to the chopped bamboo on the mountainside, then made a circle with his fingers and stuck out his thumb. Wang Fu crossed over to me with a smile.

"Dad and I set off for the mountains at eight o'clock last night," he said. "We cut down our two hundred and thirty, and then we carried thirty or forty out. I returned and wrote my composition. I finished it before midnight. It's at home now. I have an Educated Youth as witness."

He looked at the prefect. "You're the stakeholder. The dictionary ..." Wang Fu turned red, his voice dropped and trembled: "I've won."

I was speechless. I looked at Wang Fu and then at Wang Qitong.

Wang Qitong stopped his weird chuckle and resumed clearing off side-shoots. The class looked at the pile of cut bamboo and then at me.

"Well done, Wang Fu," I said.

I realized I didn't know how to express to Wang Fu how I felt.

Wang Fu was looking at the prefect. Gazing at me, she slowly took a paper parcel out of her satchel, walked over and put it in Wang Fu's hands. Wang Fu looked at me.

I sighed. "Wang Fu, I'm giving you the dictionary as a present, but not because you've won."

Wang Fu bridled. "I'll go and get my composition."

"It's not necessary. The deal we made was for you to write yesterday about today's manual labor. You did write your composition yesterday, but it was yesterday you completed the manual labor. When you record something it's always after the event, this is an irrefutable truth. But you're an extremely serious student, and you've done so much for the class I'm giving you this dictionary as a present."

The class remained silent. Wang Fu carefully opened the parcel revealing the dictionary—a small, square object. He then rewrapped the parcel in great haste and thrust it into the prefect's hands.

He looked up at me.

"I lost. I won't take it. I'll ... I'll copy the dictionary. I'll copy a little every day, fifty thousand characters, a hundred characters a day, five hundred days. We've spent eight years copying our textbooks."

I paused in silence, and replied, "Okay, you make a copy."

v

From then on Wang Fu copied the dictionary every day in my room after school. I'd often light a cigarette and sit next to him, watching him copy. Occasionally my doubts resurfaced: was I harming my students? Was this really the right way to teach? And was this really the right way to study? From the beginning I had taken teaching very seriously, and now I had made studying so rigid. What were my responsibilities as a teacher? Watching Wang Fu copy more and more each day, I nevertheless felt that I should continue teaching the children to be conscientious and honest. I was more at peace with this, though I was still worried about Wang Fu.

One day the film projection team came to the branch farm. Films were in extremely short supply in the mountains, and as a rule we only experienced this treat once a year or so. Whenever the projection team came it was naturally like a holiday in the mountains. The class talked about it the whole day, and when the last bell rang, the children who lived farther away didn't go home or bother about eating, but arrived at the screening early to get seats. I was expecting Brownie and the others from my team to visit the school, so I carried two long benches from the classroom to my own room. There I found Wang Fu sitting at my desk in the thick of his daily copying.

"Wang Fu, aren't you going early to get a seat? They're saying it's a very good film!"

"Don't worry," Wang Fu said, without raising his head. "I'm nearly finished. There's still plenty of time."

"Okay, keep copying and I'll get some dinner for us. We can eat here. After you finish and we've eaten, we can go together."

Still not raising his head, Wang Fu said, "I won't eat," and continued copying.

Brownie and the others arrived as expected, calling loudly from the dirt play area. Hurrying out I saw that they were wearing new clothes, and there were sharp creases in their pants. Laidi looked even more colorful. Her blouse and pants were very smartly cut, stretched tightly over those parts of the body a man lacks. I smiled.

"The team cookhouse lets you steal more than enough to live

on, Laidi, you don't need to spend any money on extra food. Why don't you buy some material and make yourself a blouse that's slightly roomier. What you're wearing is so skimpy it hurts just to look at you."

Laidi patted her hair.

"Pipe down! Men have such poor eyesight—and now you're suddenly as keen-sighted as an old rooster? Watch and learn. Today all the teams will be secretly trying to outdress each other. If you're still your old ma's boy, you'll back me up."

Brownie raised his head, bending it back, then collapsed his body forward until his head neared the ground and spat violently.

Laidi laughed. "Beanpole, let's have a look at your classroom."

I led everyone inside. Scanning around, they said it looked like a dog kennel. One by one they squeezed themselves behind a desk and sat down.

"Come on, Beanpole," said Brownie, "give us a lesson."

"Who's going to say 'All rise'?" I asked.

"I'll do it," said Laidi.

I walked out the door and came back in again.

"All rise!" Laidi yelled.

Brownie and the others squeezed themselves up again, pushing the desks over. Everyone burst out laughing. Together they pulled the desks upright and sat back down. I cleared my throat.

"Right, let's start. Today's lesson is extremely important, you must pay attention. I'll read the text aloud first."

Laidi patted her hair and glanced at the others. Then, with a gleam in her eyes, she fixed her gaze on me. Walking slowly in front of the blackboard, I held my index finger erect.

"Listen carefully. Once upon a time there was a mountain. And on the mountain there was a temple. And in the temple there was an old monk telling a story. What story was he telling? Once upon a time there was a mountain. And on the mountain there was a temple. And in the temple there was an old monk telling ..."

Brownie and the others solemnly shouted together, "... a story!

What story was he telling? Once upon a time there was a mountain. And on the mountain ..."

Together they repeated the lines in unison, measuring a strong beat while their voices grew louder and louder, as if they were on the mountainside making the ravines ring with their chanting.

As the noise subsided I saw it was growing dark.

"Hurry up and save some seats. I'll join you after I've eaten."

They agreed and were about to leave when Laidi said, "Brownie, save a seat for me, too. I'm going to take a peak at Beanpole's hut."

Everyone laughed. "Don't you know everything there is to know already? What more is there to see?"

"I'm going to help him make dinner," Laidi said.

"Sounds good!" they said, grinning broadly. "Cooking's the first step!" And off they went, singing.

I pointed out my door to Laidi and she went inside.

"What!" she shouted. "Are you punishing your student?"

I followed her in and found Wang Fu still copying. He hadn't even lit the lamp.

"Stop copying, Wang Fu," I said as I lit the oil lamp. "Let's eat."

Laidi looked at Wang Fu.

"So this is Wang Fu? Aren't you hard working! No wonder Beanpole keeps singing your praises. Has he given you a lot of homework?"

"No," Wang Fu said, embarrassed. "I'm copying out the teacher's dictionary."

Laidi bent her head to look.

"Fuck," she said, looking pleased, "that's my dictionary!"

As I scooped out some rice and washed it, I told Laidi why Wang Fu was copying the dictionary. She picked the book up in one hand, tossed it into the other, and passed it over to Wang Fu.

"Take it. As a present from me."

Wang Fu looked at me, slowly edged away, and squatted down

to help me with the rice.

"The dictionary was a present from her to me. Then I gave it to you and you refused to take it. Now the real owner wants to give it to you, you should accept it."

"I'll copy it," said Wang Fu softly. "Copying makes it stick in my mind. Dad said he'd see if there was a chance to transport rice to the provincial capital and try to buy a copy there, since he wasn't able to help me win it."

"Your dad?" Laidi said. "Loose…"

I glared at Laidi and the color immediately rose in her cheeks. She shot a look back at me and squeezed past us.

"Out of the way, let me do it. You two are impossibly slow."

With much banging and clanking she set to work without another word.

After we finished eating, Wang Fu wrapped his exercise books in a piece of cloth and put the bundle under his arm. Then he rushed out, saying that his father must have arrived by now.

"You go on ahead," I said to Laidi as I tidied up.

Laidi sat down. "Stop worrying. Films screened outdoors can be seen from anywhere."

I paused for a moment, then sat down on the bed. The oil lamp glowed feebly. I was starting to feel uncomfortable and tried to think of something to say. Laidi was slowly turning the pages of the dictionary. Occasionally she threw me a glance, her eyes brighter than the oil lamp. I suddenly remembered.

"I've nearly finished the words for your song," I told her cheerfully.

Laidi turned to me at once. "I thought you had forgotten. Let me have a look."

I got up, rummaged around for the sheet, and passed it over to her. I lit a cigarette and watched her. Laidi read it quickly and smiled.

"These words aren't very highbrow. I really overestimated you!"

I exhaled a mouthful of smoke and watched it snake and curl in front of the oil lamp.

"Why should they be highbrow? Plain words sung plainly are perfect for songs. You were the one who was boasting about being able to write music."

Laidi nodded. "Where's the refrain?" she asked.

"Do we need a refrain?"

"Of course we do. Write one now. Two lines is enough. I've already thought of music for the first section."

I gazed at her.

Looking very pleased with herself, Laidi rose from the chair. She walked halfway around the room, looked at me, and shouted, "Get to work!"

Provoked to action, I read the words again by the light of the oil lamp, mulled over a few phrases, jotted down two lines, and jumped up.

"Your turn now!" I ordered.

Laidi skipped over, bent her head to see, settled her bottom on the chair with a knee spread on each side of the table, and began to write, her pen scratching away.

From afar drifted the faint sound of the opening film music, the notes rising and falling. It wasn't that easy to screen a film in the mountains. You needed several men to take turns powering the generator by pedaling. Sometimes the man pedaling tired and the electricity would fluctuate, causing the sound from the loudspeakers to become slurred, distorting the well-known arias. Meanwhile on the screen, an uplifting scene of "heroic deeds" might have started boldly but would suddenly lapse into hesitation. In the mountains, though, everyone enjoyed watching anyway. Other times the man on the pedals changed the tempo on purpose, creatively improvising, and the old films would send the audience into fits of laughter.

Immersed in these thoughts, Laidi finished her composing and jumped up to show me. I tried to hum the tune and was starting to feel it when Laidi pushed me aside. "Stop squawking like an old rooster. This is how it goes ...," and she began to sing shrilly.

The song really did sound special, incorporating a musical figure from Laidi's hometown. Nice syncopations; a good swing. It would certainly sound special when the children sang it.

As Laidi sang for the second time with greater energy, the door crashed open. Brownie and the others tumbled in, hooting with laughter.

"Laidi, what are these sugar-coated cannonballs you're firing now? What will the neighbors think? You're going to get Beanpole here into big trouble."

"Why aren't you watching the film?" I asked.

"Movies come once in eight hundred years and yet they show the same old film," Brownie said. "We'd rather hang out here. Laidi, you've fizzled out—Juanzi from team five was the big star today. Someone bought her a pair of bell-bottoms at the market across the border. Apparently it's what everyone's wearing now. The pants are stretched so tight across her butt it looks like a bun split down the middle: a real eye-opener! Just as well you stayed behind or you would have lost it."

"Who cares about asses?" cried Laidi with uncharacteristic good humor. "I've written a song! I'll teach it to you. Get ready to sing, everyone."

With great enthusiasm we followed Laidi's lead and soon we bellowed out in unison:

> One, two, three, four, five
> Our last year we've really strived
> Now we've learned to read and write
> After school our future's bright
>
> Five, four, three, two, one
> Our last year is second to none;
> Each pair of shoulders supports one head
> We write what we think, not what we've read

The refrain followed with the music five notes higher. Brownie sang a little off-key and Laidi glared at him. Blushing, he stopped singing and restrained himself to slapping his thighs.

We were all in high spirits, agreeing that the song was invigorating.

"A pity the words don't measure up," Laidi observed.

I sighed and remarked that writing lyrics wasn't easy, that it was an accomplishment even to produce words that make sense. How effortless it was for me to be strict with my students day after day, like headquarters passing out production tasks. Now that my turn had come, I couldn't help sympathizing with the children, and it dawned on me that I could also liven up my teaching.

VI

The first lesson the next morning was composition. The children said the topic would surely be last night's film.

"Last night's film?" I said. "The newspapers have been commenting on it for years, what's the point of you writing about it? We've already written about lots of things, things that we've seen. So, today, write about someone you know. Human beings are complex creatures, it's difficult to describe them. But try, write what you already know. What do you already know? Think about it, and we'll discuss this more later."

"I'll write about the person who cooks for our team," said the class prefect.

"Fine."

Some of them said they wanted to write about me.

"Do you know me that well already?" I laughed. "We've only been together a couple of months. I bet you don't even know if I snore in my sleep." They laughed and I added, "Do as you like, I don't mind serving as a live target."

The children buried their heads in their exercise books. It was then that I remembered the song. As I paced slowly back and forth, I said, "Today, I want you to stay a little longer after school. I have a good song to teach you."

Their curiosity aroused, they stopped writing. I told them to finish their composition and I'd tell them about it that afternoon.

The sun peaked; the empty playground radiated light. Feeling cheerful, I stood inside the door gazing outside. Some distance away, I saw Chen cross the playground in the company of a stranger. They stopped and Chen pointed in my direction. The stranger stared at me and followed Chen into the office. I thought it was probably a friend of Chen's who was visiting, and that he was giving him a tour of the school grounds. Pigs and hens roamed around outside, releasing occasional dirty traces behind them, searching in each other's droppings for something edible. I couldn't help silently congratulating myself on being human. Imagine being an animal watched like this by human beings—it would truly be too humiliating!

Again, Wang Fu was the first to hand in his work. I held it in my hands and read it slowly. I was astonished. He wrote:

My Father

My father is one of the strongest men in the world. No one in our team can beat him at carrying sacks of rice. My father also eats more than anyone else in the world. My mother always lets him eat all the food we have. This is right, because my father has to work, and his wages support our whole family. But my father says, "I am not as strong as Wang Fu, because Wang Fu can read and write." My father isn't able to talk but I understand what he means. I know that people in the team bully him. Therefore I want to study and learn how to speak for him.

> *My father is very hard working. He was sick today, but still he climbed out of bed. He wanted to go to work so he wouldn't lose a day's pay. I have to go to school so I cannot replace him now. In the white*

morning sunshine, my father climbed the mountain. He walked into
the white sunshine. I can tell my father has got his strength back.

I stood still for a long time, then placed Wang Fu's paper down
on the desk and looked at him. His head lowered, he was writing
something, probably homework for another class, and the whorl
in his brown hair faced me. I looked out into the yard, which
shimmered in the heat. My eyes began to sting. Pressing them
shut, I wondered: could I have taught him so much?

The recess bell rang. I collected the papers and was about to head to
my room but after a moment's thought turned to the office instead.
Inside I saw Chen and the stranger sitting across from each other.

Chen beckoned me over. He pointed to the man, saying "This
is Comrade Wu from the Education Office at farm headquarters.
He has some business to discuss with you."

I looked at him and he looked at me, then he flicked off the
length of ash from the cigarette between his fingers.

"Have you been making bets with your students?"

I did not understand, but I nodded.

"What lesson are you on in class?" Comrade Wu continued.

"I'm teaching the class but I'm not using the textbook."

"Why not?"

I thought for a while. "It's useless," I finally said.

Comrade Wu looked at Chen. "You tell him."

Chen immediately said, "You tell him."

"It's perfectly clear," Comrade Wu said. "You tell him."

With eyes averted, Chen said, "Headquarters feels that you
need more training. As far as the branch farm is concerned, you
can choose another team if you don't want to return to your old
one. Personally, uhm ... I'd say you can take your time. Pass your
class to your replacement and take a break, think things over. I
suggest you join team three."

I understood at once that the matter was very simple, but I

pretended to think about it.

"It doesn't matter which team, the work's all the same. I don't need to think things over. Since I didn't use the textbook there's nothing to hand over. I'll leave right away. I'd like to take the compositions my students have written, will that be a problem?"

Chen and Comrade Wu stared at me. I gave the textbook back to Chen.

Comrade Wu hesitated a moment then passed me a cigarette.

I smiled and said, "I don't smoke."

Comrade Wu stuck the cigarette behind his ear. "Well, then, I must be getting back."

Chen earnestly shuffled the exercise books on his desk back and forth.

When I walked out of the office, the sun was scorching. I glanced over at my classroom. It was dark inside. I thought: why not go back to my team first? I left the school with the sun beating down on my head.

Early the next morning I came back to collect my things. Leaving the bamboo bed mats on the bed frame, I carried my bags through the heavy mist along the mountain path to team three. As before, the sun was a white disc. I stopped mid-stride, took the dictionary out of my bag, opened it, and wrote carefully: "To Wang Fu, from Laidi." Then I added my name next to hers.

Slowly I walked on again, instinctively beginning to relax.

AFTERWORD

T o Chinese readers and writers, the year 1984 was one of celebration. The strictest censorship in arts and letters since
the Cultural Revolution (1966–1976) had been imposed in the late
summer of 1983, as Deng Xiaoping's campaign against "spiritual pollution" threatened ever harsher penalties against non-
conformist writers and artists. By the spring of 1984, however,
the campaign had faltered, and that summer it was superseded
by promises of relaxation in literature and the arts. The most remarkable new writer was Ah Cheng, author of three stories that
presented with detached irony and unexpected good humor some
fundamental characteristics of modern Chinese life, its minor
triumphs as well as its prolonged suffering.

Zhong Acheng, better known under his pen name Ah Cheng, was born in 1949, a few months before Mao Zedong proclaimed the founding of the People's Republic of China. During the early post-Liberation days, his family was part of Beijing's intellectual and political elite. His father, Zhong Dianfei, was a prominent film theorist and academic, whose hobbies included the study of the Daoist classic *Zhuangzi*; his mother held a clerical position in the Beijing Film Studio. Zhong, whose membership in the Chinese Communist Party went back to the 1940s, was also in charge of the film section of the Communist Party's Propaganda Bureau, writing reports on each new film as it appeared. In late 1956, as part of the Hundred Flowers campaign initiated by Mao Zedong to curb party power and privilege, Zhong wrote a strongly worded criticism of bureaucratic and political interference in contemporary films. Artists and intellectuals praised the article, but in the campaign against "Rightists" that followed, Zhong was suspended from his job and sent to the countryside for "reform through labor."

With an elderly mother and five small children to support, his wife resorted to desperate measures in order to survive. Ah Cheng, the second eldest child, was given the task of selling his father's library of Chinese and foreign books. Previously, the children had been forbidden to touch these books, which were locked up in glass bookcases. Now, every time Ah Cheng was given a bundle of books to sell, he would sneak them up to his room to read them first. Along with the great novels of traditional China like *The Water Margin* and *Dream of the Red Chamber*, he read translations of works by Tolstoy, Balzac, Dostoyevsky, and Hugo while still in his early teens.

Zhong Dianfei's position was restored in the early 1960s, and it was probably through family influence that Ah Cheng was able to enroll in the Beijing Fourth High School, attended by children of top leaders such as Liu Shaoqi. Fellow pupils whose later careers were to touch his included Bei Dao, China's leading poet in exile, and Chen Kaige, one of China's most famous film directors. Ah Cheng's chance for a solid if Russian-style education and guaranteed entry into the elite seemed even more secure when he entered senior secondary school in September 1965. The Cultural Revolution broke out at the end of the school year, however, and the power enjoyed by the old alliance of political and intellectual elites began to fail as the social hostility that this alliance had provoked was exploited by a faction of party radicals. Bureaucrats and intellectuals like Zhong Dianfei were deposed, their families were broken up and subjected to harsh "re-education," and their children faced a bleak future as schools closed down in 1966. All this is briefly described at the beginning of "The King of Chess."

One of the Cultural Revolution's main forms of social engineering was the mass movement to send "educated youth" (secondary school boys and girls) from the cities to the countryside in 1968. Most of rural China was at this time divided into communes, representing collective ownership by the local peasantry. Parallel to the communes were the state farms, owned by successive tiers of local (county & district), provincial, and national government. The state farms were semi-military in character, often placed along national borders or associated with prison or labor camps. State farm headquarters were usually located in an existing market town or larger village that might also serve as the local administrative center. The area covered by the state farm was divided into branch farms, corresponding to existing villages, and further subdivided into teams often located in remoter areas with few inhabitants. A primary school might be found in a branch farm serving several teams, but secondary schools only existed at the county town or district level, and universities were restricted to provincial capitals. The practical work of the teams was supervised by a team leader, but the branch party secretary had responsibility for the general conduct of the team members. The teenagers who were sent to the countryside were often assigned to state farms, where they could be supervised while having little contact with local village life. It was noticed, but not commented on in public, that this clashed with one of the stated aims of the policy: to subject urban youth to "re-education" by the peasantry.

Ah Cheng was first sent to a village in Shanxi in the northwest. He had been fond of drawing since childhood, and finding little inspiration in the barren countryside around him, he was beguiled by a friend's tales of the grasslands into transferring to Inner Mongolia to sketch cattle and sheep. Life in yurts turned out less romantic than he had expected. Yunnan, China's southwest province, offered more luxuriant subjects, and Ah Cheng ended up in a state farm along the Laotian border in the mountains of Xishuangbanna, in the remotest part of Yunnan. Ah Cheng spent the next few years here in a forlorn effort to grow rubber where foreign geographers had claimed that rubber could not be cultivated. (Chen Kaige was located a mountain or two to the east.)

Excluded even from daily village life, the displaced youth regarded themselves as stranded in a cultural desert, with little entertainment apart from playing cards and gambling. The nights in Xishuangbanna were not illuminated by electricity; instead, under a tree in summer and huddled inside for warmth in winter, Ah Cheng enlivened the long evening hours by the light of an oil lamp recounting the stories he had read at school or in his father's books. He quickly found out that storytelling was also a way to improve his material circumstances, especially if he widened his audience to include the local villagers. As Ah Cheng learnt to adapt his storytelling to traditional expectations, precious food and cigarettes were pressed on him. He eventually became so popular that he could pick his own audience according to who offered the best meal. He also became more daring in his choice of subject matter, relying on the distance of these village families from local centers of political power. One of his last efforts was a version of *Anna Karenina*, adapted to traditional Chinese customs and morality, in short segments over several months; when the same audiences saw the British television version on Chinese national TV in 1984, some of them were angry with Ah Cheng for having deceived them with his adaptation.

As the Cultural Revolution abated in the early 1970s, Ah Cheng won a transfer to Kunming, the scenic but impoverished capital of Yunnan, where he worked for some years in the local cultural bureaucracy. He was allowed home leave once a year, and one of his visits to Beijing coincided with the Tiananmen demonstrations of April 1976, when attempts to disperse attendance at a memorial gathering for Zhou Enlai provoked massive protests which resulted in the overthrow of the Gang of Four later the same year. Ah Cheng took part in the demonstrations, and a sketch he had made of Zhou Enlai was widely copied and circulated. Many of the demonstrators were urban youth who had managed to transfer back home to Beijing in the mid-1970s, but Ah Cheng had to return to Yunnan.

Following Mao Zedong's death in 1976, the next few years were proving the liveliest since Liberation. Political reformers and the political underground, literary reformists and the literary underground, all seemed to have a common interest in challenging the conventions that had ruled China since 1949. On Beijing's Democracy Wall, former underground publications became the basis of an unofficial press. In sympathy with the political aims of the Democratic Movement, Bei Dao and friends founded an unofficial literary magazine, *Today*, in November 1978, featuring modernist poetry and fiction written in secret since the early 1970s. One of the contributors was Chen Kaige, who was now a student at the Beijing Film Academy, while Ah Cheng's sketch of Zhou Enlai was featured in the first issue.

Ah Cheng's transfer to Beijing finally took place in 1979 when he was given a job as a magazine art editor, his duties including journalism, layout, and illustration. In Yunnan, he had met a talented young woman who returned to Beijing some years earlier to study and now worked as a teacher at the Languages Institute. With both of them earning money, they were able to marry and moved into a small house in the northern inner suburbs. Later he changed jobs to assist his father, then editor-in-chief of a film journal, and moved into the grounds of Beijing Film Studio where Chen Kaige lived with his parents.

In Beijing Ah Cheng continued to entertain friends with tales of life in Xishuangbanna, and before long these tales made their way into print. "The King of Chess" was published in the July issue of the nationally circulated *Shanghai Literature* in 1984. The immediate critical reaction was highly favorable, and the story became the sensation of the season. Official acceptance was signified by an article in *Literary News* (the journal of the Chinese Writers' Association) in October, praising the story for its portrayal of the twin virtues of the life of the mind and life among the people, with a light rebuke for the Chess King's individualism. In December the story won a national award, and Ah Cheng felt secure enough to exchange his salaried job in a state organization for greater opportunity in the private sector and to concentrate on his writing.

As offers from editors around the country poured in and reporters besieged the new celebrity, the Writers' Association arranged for Ah Cheng to spend a month in one of its guesthouses to write his next story. "The King of Trees" was published in the inaugural issue of *Chinese Writers* in January 1985; "The King of Children" appeared a few months later in the country's leading literary journal, *People's Literature*. The three King stories plus two shorter stories were published as a book in Hong Kong in October 1985, and a wider selection of Ah Cheng's work followed in Beijing in November. A pirated edition of the Hong Kong book with additional critical essays was published in Taipei in August 1986 and reprinted the next year. Chen Kaige, buoyed by the huge success of his first film *The Yellow Earth* in 1984, decided to adapt "The King of Children" for his third film in the summer of 1986, and it was released in Cannes in 1988. Ah Cheng in the meantime had been engaged by several film studios as a scriptwriter and designer, but despite several tentative moves, neither of the other two stories has yet been filmed.

II

The popularity of Ah Cheng's three stories is a tribute to the breadth of their appeal. Cultural bureaucrats welcomed the uncomplaining, even cheerful attitude of the writer toward the material and mental suffering engendered by mistaken party policies. Chinese intellectuals at home and abroad appreciated the complex vocabulary that gives bones and sinew to the apparently artless style, the linguistic borrowings from traditional Chinese novels dating back to Ming and Qing, and the references to Daoist philosophy. Ah Cheng's own generation relished the honest evocation of those fateful years; in his stories, poverty and deprivation are lightly veiled in nostalgia for the simplicity and comradeship of those days, which had disappeared amid the conflicts of a rapidly modernizing society. Puritans approved the message that material needs and sensual satisfaction might be reduced to their most austere levels. Patriots and conformists were heartened by the lack of obviously Western-derived techniques used by modernist writers and by the rich subtext of traditional Chinese thought and expression. Environmentalists and traditionalist art-lovers greeted the victory of ecological pantheism over humanist realism. Political and literary dissidents, along with many foreign sinologists, focused on the subversive aspects of the stories: between the lines, the stories seemed to suggest the ultimate futility of politics in people's lives. Critics in Taiwan uncovered evidence of disillusion with Communist rule.

Over time, Ah Cheng's stories became invested with new significance. As memories of the Cultural Revolution faded, the stories became witness to events that are still too sensitive for open public debate in China. From a different perspective, they point to attitudes and customs that have persisted throughout the whole modern period, not just the Cultural Revolution or the early post-Liberation years. The key themes in the stories, from spiritual freedom to fun, from environmental concerns to social relations, are also relevant to contemporary readers around the world.

Ah Cheng left China for the U.S. in 1978, where he supported himself for a while as a housepainter. He was outspoken during the events of spring 1989, when his uncompromising stance re-aligned him with other involuntary exiles such as Bei Dao. He now lives in the countryside near Beijing, making a living as a screenwriter as well as at other unspecified jobs. He continues to write, although not much is published and neither he nor his work comes much under media scrutiny. Serious critics and scholars nevertheless hold his work in the highest regard. Ah Cheng himself still prefers to tell stories at literary conferences instead of delivering speeches, remaining aloof from debates on his work or on the nature and future of Chinese literature. He maintains that he writes to supplement his income, that his skills are those of a carpenter, and that problems of creative freedom are not his concern.

III

The commentary by the narrator of "The King of Chess" makes it clear that the story is not about chess (Ah Cheng claims that he doesn't even know how to play) but about the cultivation of a certain way of life: both narrator and protagonist emerge at the end of the story with a new understanding of life's meaning. The philosophical basis of this meaning is left vague, but references to Daoism throughout give an indication of the author's orientation.

Daoism is a complex system of reasoning and belief with many variants, but it can be grouped among those schools of thought and religion that offer solace to those disappointed or rejected by the mundane world. The first overt reference to Daoism in "The King of Chess" comes in the explanation of chess strategy given by one of the two elderly chess masters. The first is a wastepaper collector, the second a scholarly recluse; both live outside society, and their wisdom does not lend itself to Confucian service of the state. A third example is taken from history: the scholar Ni Yunlin from the Yuan dynasty, who becomes a chess master during a period of social unrest when he is forced to leave his estate and take to the back roads, is claimed as an ancestor by the fictional Ni Bin. The father of a schoolmate, on the other hand, a chess master who conforms to social pressures, is shown as an inferior player as well as a pompous timeserver.

Flight from urban life can have its positive aspects. To a Daoist, the countryside is not a place of reluctant exile but a refuge where the original simplicity and dignity of life may be rediscovered. Accompanying their physical removal from urban life, Ah Cheng's protagonists experience mental escape as well. Adapting a line from an old Chinese poem, the Chess King, Wang Yisheng, is fond of saying "How may one dispel melancholy? Only by chess." The game of chess here represents the minor traditions in Chinese culture, dedication to artistic and intellectual pursuits, and an enjoyment to be shared with friends. In contrast, the more refined aspects of high culture are shown to be of little value. Wang Yisheng's mother was a prostitute and he never knew his father, but he easily defeats Ni Bin whose family is famous for its cultivation of elite aesthetic pleasures. Traditional Chinese painting also appears as a commodity to be employed for corrupt purposes. Genuinely creative art, in contrast, is signified by a bohemian painter's sketches of naked bodies in motion. The painter and Wang Yisheng also share a sense of pleasure in their respective vocations. Although the game amounts to a punishing discipline when Wang Yisheng over-extends himself, he normally enjoys playing. This atmosphere of fun and leisure in the story was rare in modern Chinese literature, with its history of high seriousness.

In another aspect, however, Wang Yisheng is shown as being more aware of the basics of life than other urban youth, thanks to his early exposure to poverty. The importance given to food in the story, unprecedented in modern Chinese fiction, is an accurate indicator of conditions in China during the 1960s and 1970s. Material deprivation in the countryside made food more important in the lives of urban youth and sharpened their appreciation of simple fare. Chess and food—playing and eating—are the two poles between which the story is constructed. The wastepaper collector warns Wang Yisheng that chess cannot serve as a livelihood, and at the end of the story, he rejects official honors and status. For the greater part of the story, the distance between the two poles in his life places him in a precarious situation.

Wang Yisheng is rescued from this situation by his new-found ability to relax in the company of friends. The sufferings and betrayals of those years gave added meaning to loyalty, sincerity, and shared hardship, and many middle-aged Chinese people still look back in nostalgia to the close friendships formed at that time. The joint satisfaction of friendship and hunger at the snake-meat feast in "The King of Chess" is one of the most notable scenes in contemporary Chinese fiction. Happiness is neither the proletarian joys of labor and making revolution, nor the decadent pleasures of the bourgeoisie, but a simple meal with friends. In modern China, this commonplace is less trite than it sounds. At the end of the story, the narrator has gained a new respect for the potential of spiritual release in mental discipline and the true values of life among working people (as distinct from urban entertainment and high culture), while the protagonist emerges with greater appreciation of the necessity of friendship in even the most dissociated life: a chess fool becomes the Chess King.

Although life was grim for these urban youth, their distance from political centers and the satisfaction of basic needs (food, shelter, and paid employment) by the state gave them a curious kind of freedom and security. While most fiction about this period shows urban youth as the frail victims of political forces beyond their reach, Wang Yisheng, on the contrary, controls his own life and is master of his fate. He is impatient at his friends' self-pity: most of the urban youth had only been demoted from social privilege to living standards closer to the vast majority of the population. Nevertheless, one political dimension in Wang Yisheng's sense of social justice is disturbing.

At issue is the implication in "The Chess King" that spiritual escape by the exercise of mental discipline was a possible life choice available to urban youth. On one reading, Ah Cheng asserts the invincibility of the human spirit in the face of material deprivation and political oppression. Chen Kaige once compared Bei Dao and Ah Cheng as follows: Bei Dao became famous for the line "I do not believe"; Ah Cheng would have written "I believe." In other words, Ah Cheng's apparently simple-minded acceptance of the world is ultimately more subversive than open dissent. Other readers find Ah Cheng's "spiritual victories" as spurious as Ah Q's (Lu Xun's famous non-hero of the early Republican period). At the height of political repression during the Cultural Revolution, when the main events of these stories took place, almost any non-"revolutionary" activity was automatically anti-revolutionary. Wang Yisheng is pressed into a statement that even though a capricious authority may prevent him from playing chess openly, it could never prevent him from doing so in his mind. Many readers have wondered at the naïveté of this statement, which is left unchallenged in the story. It is true, though often unacknowledged, that for many people the Cultural Revolution was merely an unpleasant or even occasionally enjoyable passage in their lives that could be endured and forgotten. For many others, however, innocent or not, it brought beatings, rape, imprisonment, torture, and execution. Both official and modernist critics condemn Ah Cheng's escapism, whether this escapism occurs in the immediate past (the time-setting of the stories) or the present (when the stories were written and published); both demanded that writers must come more directly to grips with the problems of a modernizing society. The wastepaper collector claims that the discarded paper he collects can be sorted out, sold, and used to support his life and serve new purposes. Modernists and political dissidents have denied the possibility of ideological recycling.

IV

Values in "The King of Trees" and "The King of Children" are generally more specific and explicit than in "The King of Chess." Some critics have also claimed a decline in literary quality and imaginative power, but over succeeding decades each of these two has won its own champions. There are several references to Daoism in "The King of Trees," where an old soldier's instinctive environmentalism becomes concrete in a supernatural fusion of man's fate with nature itself. The wider message is contained in the narrator's vague but growing rejection of both the anti-Daoist Cultural Revolution slogan "Man can conquer Heaven/Nature" and post-1949 manifestations of Confucian rote-learning and moralizing. In the same story, however, the moral harshness displayed by the soldier is more Confucian than Daoist, and his loyalty, remorse, and honorable poverty are described so as to engage the reader's sympathy. "The King of Children" is similarly ambivalent: the new teacher's emphasis on creative writing is in accord with modern Western thinking and also compatible with Daoism, while the respect given to dictionaries represents a much older adherence to Confucianism. In traditional China, a scholar could well espouse Confucian or Daoist values at different times in his life; it might be expected that Confucian elements would emerge in the stories that Ah Cheng published after his promotion to official celebrity in 1984.

All three stories, however, reject the official political and moral values of the Cultural Revolution. Ah Cheng frequently achieves this effect by negative references to the sun—the official and dominant image for Mao Zedong in Cultural Revolution iconography—and other familiar images or names of the period, such as "the Great Helmsman" in "The King of Trees." In "The King of

Chess," the worn red banners and the broadcast songs based on quotations from Mao are ignored in the confusion at the train station where the urban youth depart for exile; in "The King of Trees," the giant primeval tree is cut down because it "hides the sun so that other things can't grow"; and in "The King of Children," the hardworking peasant recovers from his illness and walks out into the white sun—not the "red sun" of Mao Zedong.

v

Ah Cheng's stories are unusually dense in reference to contemporary and traditional Chinese culture. The language is similarly complex, combining colloquial Chinese with vocabulary from contemporary political jargon and older traditional fiction. Ah Cheng's style also incorporates other features of traditional storytelling, such as the single-stranded chronological narration in which earlier events are related only through extended dialogue, and the implied presence of an audience. The narrator in two of the stories is an observer whose conversational mode creates the illusion that he is addressing a live audience, while the tone of "The King of Children" is slightly more reflective and literary, as if the first-person protagonist is making a written record of his experience. In all three stories, the dialogue is differentiated from the narrative, distinguishing the locality and class of characters such as Wang Yisheng's stepfather (Beijing working class), Tall Balls (Shanghai elite), Laidi (Shanghai working class), and Knotty (southern soldier turned farmer).

Unlike contemporary modernist fiction, there are few references to Western literature in the stories, and little use of modernist techniques such as interior monologue and time shifts. The sole direct mentions of Western literature are made by the narrator in "The King of Chess," who has read Jack London's "Love of Life" and stories by Balzac (as would be normal for bright Chinese schoolboys in the 1950s and early 1960s). Ah Cheng's stories have several features in common with London's: a preoccupation with material deprivation, physical suffering, and endurance, a detailed description of gestures, a celebration of male companionship, a fascination with the life and mentality of people living in poor, remote areas, and the spiritual significance of all of these things. A Chinese ancestor of the same kind, one of the few traditional works mentioned in the story by name, is the seventeenth century novel of loyal banditry, *Water Margin*.

References to contemporary Chinese culture are more common. For example, the "revolutionary model theatrical works" which dominated cultural life during the Cultural Revolution are mentioned several times. The performance at the end of "The King of Chess" was probably a model opera, and model opera is also mentioned in "The King of Trees." Li Tiemei, the unintentionally glamorous subject of a poster in "The King of Children," is the young heroine from the model opera *The Red Lantern*, and the movies that Beanpole and the others watch are filmed versions of the model works. Although the model works were subjected to heavy criticism immediately after the Cultural Revolution, they represent a significant attempt to modernize traditional Chinese theater and were quite popular at the time: their rigidity as "models" and their small number in endless performance were the chief reasons for audience hostility.

More irritating perhaps than the literary and artistic works foisted on the population by the radical faction in power during the Cultural Revolution was the constant stream of jargon which announced new policies: the unnatural or even perverted terminology added insult to the injury of the policies themselves. The jargon soon became part of everyday conversation, but the stiffness still attached to these terms make the children's dialogue simultaneously saddening and absurd. The main characters in the stories are schoolchildren who are not at school. All schools were closed down during the early years of the Cultural Revolution, and universities did not reopen until the 1970s. Primary school was reduced from six years to five when schools started up again, but the uneven structure of secondary schools was retained: most children completed the three years of junior high school, but only a small number of city children had the opportunity to enter the two years of senior high school and qualify for university. In the countryside, teachers were often barely better educated than the children they taught.

Ah Cheng's description of people's gestures is a remarkable feature of his narrative style. These gestures were both very common in contemporary Chinese life and also very revealing of the character's states of mind and social position. By relying on this kind of external description in a way typical of traditional Chinese fiction, Ah Cheng manages to deliver a great deal of information in an apparently casual and objective way, so although at times some long strings of verbs seem to slow down the action, they also provide a record of a style of life that few city people now have experienced.

References in the stories to sexual relations between these teenagers in remote areas are few and indirect, but readers should not assume that abstinence is implied. In "The King of Children," the narrator observes a cock trying to mount a hen in the schoolyard and is disappointed not to have witnessed whether the attempt was successful or not, his own coupling with Laidi can be guessed at from their friends' jibes. References to drinking alcohol are also discreet. Licensing laws were few and mostly ignored, especially outside the cities, and all sorts of fermented and distilled liquor were readily available. Still, public drunkenness remained relatively rare.

Other customs and practices recorded in these stories make up a reliable and comprehensive picture of life in those years, but not all has changed. It is still the case, for instance, that Chinese terms of address almost invariably show relative status: only close friends refer to each other by their personal names, while people with rank or in the professions are normally addressed by their title. Friends and acquaintances without rank or of approximately equivalent rank are usually addressed by their surnames prefixed by either *lao* (old) or *xiao* (young). Relatives address each other in terms of complex kinship relations: children address adults outside the family as "aunt" or "uncle" or "grandma" and "grandpa," while adults address children as "little friend." Greetings and leave-takings still differ from Western practices: it is more informal to say "I'm going" than "goodbye"; it is more common to inquire if one has eaten than about the state of one's health.

⌘

The verbal richness and subtlety of Ah Cheng's fiction have made it uncommonly difficult to translate. The complete text has been revised for this new translation, which is designed for readers with little or no Chinese or expertise in Chinese history and culture. The texts on which these translations are based are from *A Cheng xiaoshuo* (Stories by Ah Cheng), Zuojia chubanshe, Beijing, 1985. I am grateful to Chen Maiping for the three-year loan of his autographed copy of this book.

I wish to thank Ren Xiaoping for her assistance in preparing a rough draft of "The King of Children" and Zhang Nanbing for his assistance in preparing a rough draft of "The King of Trees" and also for his assistance with "The King of Chess." I am most grateful to Chen Maiping, Mi Qiu, Ah Cheng, Anders Hansson, and Halvor Eifring for their help with the translation and afterword. Guido Waldman's patient advice and tactful improvements to the English translation were invaluable. I am also grateful to the following for their advice, assistance, and encouragement in arranging publication of this book: Bei Dao, Anders Hansson, Cecilia Ip Lo Sau-shan, Peter Jay, Jeffrey Yang, and Guido Waldman.

BONNIE S. MCDOUGALL
Oslo, February 1989 /
Hong Kong, November 2009

New Directions Paperbooks—a partial listing

Henry Miller, The Air-Conditioned Nightmare
Big Sur & The Oranges of Hieronymus Bosch
The Colossus of Maroussi

Yukio Mishima, Confessions of a Mask
Death in Midsummer

Eugenio Montale, Selected Poems*

Vladimir Nabokov, Laughter in the Dark
Nikolai Gogol
The Real Life of Sebastian Knight

Pablo Neruda, The Captain's Verses*
Love Poems*
Residence on Earth*

Charles Olson, Selected Writings

George Oppen, New Collected Poems (with CD)

Wilfred Owen, Collected Poems

Michael Palmer, Thread

Nicanor Parra, Antipoems*

Boris Pasternak, Safe Conduct

Kenneth Patchen
Memoirs of a Shy Pornographer

Octavio Paz, Selected Poems
A Tale of Two Gardens

Victor Pelevin
The Hall of the Singing Caryatids
Omon Ra

Saint-John Perse, Selected Poems

Ezra Pound, The Cantos
New Selected Poems and Translations
Personae

Raymond Queneau, Exercises in Style

Qian Zhongshu, Fortress Besieged

Raja Rao, Kanthapura

Herbert Read, The Green Child

Kenneth Rexroth, Songs of Love, Moon & Wind
Written on the Sky: Poems from the Japanese

Keith Ridgway, Hawthorn & Child

Rainer Maria Rilke
Poems from the Book of Hours

Arthur Rimbaud, Illuminations*
A Season in Hell and The Drunken Boat*

Guillermo Rosales, The Halfway House

Evelio Rosero, The Armies
Good Offices

Joseph Roth, The Emperor's Tomb

Jerome Rothenberg, Triptych

Ihara Saikaku, The Life of an Amorous Woman

William Saroyan
The Daring Young Man on the Flying Trapeze

Albertine Sarrazin, Astragal

Jean-Paul Sartre, Nausea
The Wall

Delmore Schwartz
In Dreams Begin Responsibilities

W. G. Sebald, The Emigrants
The Rings of Saturn
Vertigo

Aharon Shabtai, J'accuse

Hasan Shah, The Dancing Girl

C. H. Sisson, Selected Poems

Gary Snyder, Turtle Island

Muriel Spark, The Ballad of Peckham Rye
A Far Cry From Kensington
Memento Mori

George Steiner, My Unwritten Books

Antonio Tabucchi, Indian Nocturne
Pereira Declares

Yoko Tawada, The Bridegroom Was a Dog
The Naked Eye

Dylan Thomas, A Child's Christmas in Wales
Collected Poems
Under Milk Wood

Uwe Timm, The Invention of Curried Sausage

Charles Tomlinson, Selected Poems

Tomas Tranströmer
The Great Enigma: New Collected Poems

Leonid Tsypkin, The Bridge over the Neroch
Summer in Baden-Baden

Tu Fu, Selected Poems

Frederic Tuten, The Adventures of Mao

Paul Valéry, Selected Writings

Enrique Vila-Matas, Bartleby & Co.
Dublinesque

Elio Vittorini, Conversations in Sicily

Rosmarie Waldrop, Driven to Abstraction

Robert Walser, The Assistant
Microscripts
The Tanners

Eliot Weinberger, An Elemental Thing
Oranges and Peanuts for Sale

Nathanael West
Miss Lonelyhearts & The Day of the Locust

Tennessee Williams, Cat on a Hot Tin Roof
The Glass Menagerie
A Streetcar Named Desire

William Carlos Williams, In the American Grain
Selected Poems
Spring and All

Louis Zukofsky, "A"
Anew

*BILINGUAL EDITION

For a complete listing, request a free catalog from New Directions, 80 8th Avenue, NY NY 10011
or visit us online at ndbooks.com